Also by Jonas Karlsson

The Invoice

The Room

The Circus

The Circus

A Novel

Jonas Karlsson

Hogarth
London / New York

Translation copyright © 2019 by Neil Smith

Published in the United States by Hogarth, an imprint of Random House,
a division of Penguin Random House LLC, New York.

HOGARTH is a trademark of the Random House Group Limited, and
the H colophon is a trademark of Penguin Random House LLC.

Originally published in Swedish in Sweden as *Cirkus*, based on a text
included in the collection *Den perfekta vännen*, by Wahlström & Widstrand,
2009, copyright © 2017 by Jonas Karlsson. This translation was
originally published in the United Kingdom as part of *The Room,
The Invoice, and The Circus,* published by Vintage Books,
an imprint of Penguin Random House UK, London, in 2019.

Published by agreement with The Salomonsson Agency, Stockholm.

LIBRARY OF CONGRESS CATALOGING-IN-PUBLICATION DATA
Names: Karlsson, Jonas, 1971- author. |
Smith, Neil (Neil Andrew), translator.
Title: The circus : a novel / Jonas Karlsson,
[translated from the Swedish by Neil Smith]
Other titles: Cirkus. English
Description: First edition. | London ; New York : Hogarth, [2020]
Identifiers: LCCN 2019036634 (print) | LCCN 2019036635 (ebook) |
ISBN 9781101905173 (hardcover) | ISBN 9781101905180 (ebook)
Classification: LCC PT9877.21.A74 C5713 2020 (print) |
LCC PT9877.21.A74 (ebook) | DDC 839.73/8—dc23
LC record available at https://lccn.loc.gov/2019036634
LC ebook record available at https://lccn.loc.gov/2019036635

Printed in the United States of America on acid-free paper.

randomhousebooks.com

9 8 7 6 5 4 3 2 1

First U.S. Edition

Book design by Virginia Norey

The Circus

1

It all started with the usual discussion: is it possible to be friends with someone who listens to "Fix You" by Coldplay? Then it broadened out and turned into a debate about friends and friendship in general. For a while I thought there was something wrong with the phone, like when you get a crossed line and find yourself talking to someone else. Dansson had told me you could find yourself talking to a complete stranger. Obviously I should have learned never to trust Dansson. Nor Jallo, come to that. Look, I'm getting this all muddled up. I'm not actually sure what order things happened in, to be honest. But I do know what happened. What happened when Magnus Gabrielsson disappeared at the circus. And by that I don't mean he got lost in the crowd. I mean he disappeared and didn't come back.

2

An old friend of mine, Magnus, had called me and asked if I wanted to go to the circus with him. I didn't particularly like circuses, but Magnus said this one was worth going to.

"They've got clowns," he said.

I was standing in front of my record collection holding my phone between my ear and my shoulder. In one hand I had Fun Boy Three, and in the other one of Terry Hall's solo albums, which I was trying to squeeze in between the albums by the Specials and those by the Special AKA.

I'd already spent all morning lying on Jallo's couch, drinking coffee and talking crap about all sorts of stuff. Music, old memories, the usual gossip. On and on we went. The atmosphere was pretty strained right from the start, and by the end we'd fallen out badly. It began with a discussion of "Fix You" by Coldplay, but soon developed into a wider debate about "real friends."

"So what is a 'real friend,' then?" Jallo asked, scratching his chin.

The whole thing was ridiculous. I had no desire to get bogged down in that sort of pseudo-philosophical nonsense. And the question sounded like a bit of a guilt trip. Are you a real friend? What do you mean, a *real* friend?

"Maybe your real friends aren't always the ones you think they are," Jallo went on, and started talking about a bully from back at school called Dennis, who had the worst music taste in the world.

"We become new people all the time," Jallo said.

"What do you mean by that?"

"We change. There's nothing weird about it."

In the end I got so angry that I stood up and shouted at him. I slammed the door behind me and walked all the way home. Right now all I wanted was to be left alone for a while.

Magnus went on talking about the circus, about the different acts. He gave me a long spiel about who was doing what, and what order it would be happening in. I was only half-listening, and let him go on while I sorted my records and checked that they were grouped together properly. Madness next to the Selecter next to the Specials next to Elvis Costello. Lucinda Williams next to Jolie Holland next to M. Ward next to She & Him. When Magnus noticed I still sounded dubious, he added, as if he'd suddenly remembered, "My treat, obviously."

Magnus Gabrielsson always made me feel guilty. We were old childhood friends and nowadays only met up every couple of years out of duty. We'd sit and stare at each other in awkward silence, saying it was good to see each other, that we really must do this more often, that we ought to go bowling sometime. Then we would go our separate ways, relieved that we didn't have to go through that again for another year or so.

I suppose we still had a few things in common. Music, of course, but there were other things that made us both a bit different. Neither of us had bothered to get a mobile phone, for instance. Not out of any particular point of principle—I was actually one of the first to get a cordless phone—but when mobiles appeared for some reason I never caught up. Suddenly everybody had one. And getting one then would mean being last. So neither Magnus nor I bothered. That's made things a bit difficult, and to be honest I have thought about getting one, but it's become a matter of saving face now. So we called each other on our landlines. Just less and less often. It had been over a year since we last spoke, and now he wanted me to go to the circus with him.

I thought about all the things I'd rather do: look round record shops, rent a film, browse the latest IKEA catalogue, poke about on the Ginza music website, clean the bathroom, do the sudoku in yesterday's paper. Or just carry on sorting my records. After thinking about it for a while, I decided I'd go. Not because I wanted to, but because it felt like a good opportunity to get a meeting with Magnus out of the way. Maybe that discussion about "real friends" had something to do with it as well.

3

The circus was called Hansen and Larsen's Magic Com-
pany, and it was more of a theatrical "happening" than a
traditional circus. We passed a big neon sign on which
bright red and yellow letters lit up one at a time, from the
top down, until you realized that the letters formed a top
hat. I was following Magnus. A band was already playing
when we arrived, but the whole thing felt shabby, haphaz-
ard, and not particularly well organized. The woman standing by the entrance was busy with her mobile phone. She
didn't even look up when we showed our tickets. We headed
down a corridor made of bright orange curtains, walking on
a cheap, crumpled blue carpet. A string of lights ran along
one side of the carpet, curling around itself in places. You
had to take care not to trip over it. Scattered around were
things that had clearly been taken from someone's living
room: a dresser, a standard lamp with a fabric shade, an
extension cord running across a handwoven carpet. It all
helped reinforce the illusion that we were indoors, even
though we were outside. I was already regretting coming
because the moment we entered the main arena I started

humming Frank Sinatra's "Love and Marriage," and whenever I get that stuck in my head I always know things are going to turn out badly. It's like a premonition, a way for my subconscious to let my conscious mind know that something isn't right.

The tent wasn't very big, and felt cramped and homespun, with draped material forming tunnels leading off in different directions. The floor sloped. Everything sloped. Even though there wasn't much room it was full of people, but somehow Magnus and I still managed to get good seats. In the middle of one of the benches, fairly close to the front.

The lights dimmed to leave a spotlight shining on a little red velvet curtain. Magnus stretched out beside me, tapping his foot and very excited. Almost as if he was nervous. Like a child. I wondered if maybe he'd never been to a circus before. I'd been a couple of times when I was little. Even if they were nothing like this one.

The ringmaster welcomed us all and I wondered if he was Hansen or Larsen. He waved a staff in front of our faces. I could smell the acrid stench of his old tailcoat when he raised his arm.

The ringmaster introduced a trapeze artist, supposedly the best in Europe, and she entered the ring to loud applause. The trapeze artist turned out to be a very sturdy woman with a mane of hair and big muscles. She spun some plates with cakes and pastries on them while she was balancing on the wire. But the wire was only suspended a few centimeters above the ground, so they might as well not have bothered. It could have even touched the ground as she walked along it. Either way, the audience was very enthusiastic. Magnus clapped several times, even in the middle of the act. After the trapeze artist two clowns in blue hats came in and started to build a tower out of old musical instruments while a third clown in a red hat sabotaged their efforts. They had planned the routine very cleverly so that the first two clowns never saw the third. None of them saw the others, because as soon as one went out the other two came in, and so on. The clown in the red hat hid behind the instruments and kept rearranging things when the others had left the ring. When he had wound the other two up so much that they started shouting at each other, he switched strategy and began to help them instead, and without any of them seeming to realize how it happened, in the end they succeeded in building some sort of tower. The clowns in the blue hats shook hands and congratulated each other while the clown in the red hat toppled the whole thing over and the instruments fell to the ground with a great crash. The first two clowns chased each other out of the ring with rubber mallets.

The whole act made me feel uncomfortable. But Magnus and the children in front of me laughed so hard they could hardly breathe. Magnus looked at me, but I just shook my head.

After the clowns the ringmaster came back in to introduce a magician.

"Ladies and gentlemen," he said. "I present to you Mr. Magic Bobbi!"

Bobbi was wearing a long cape and dazzling white gloves. He started off with some tricks involving rabbits and doves and playing cards, all the things magicians usually do. Then, after a while, he pulled off his gloves and said he was going to make a member of the audience disappear. He asked for a volunteer. A deafening silence followed, and I wondered if anyone was going to offer themselves. Then I realized that Magnus was raising his hand right next to my head. Everyone turned to look at us.

The magician pointed at Magnus and gestured to him to come forward. I tugged gently at his jacket but he just grinned and stood up.

When Magnus reached him, the magician asked what Magnus's name was, and he told him, speaking into a red microphone.

"So, Magnus, what do you think about being spirited away?" the magician asked, and the audience laughed.

"No problem," Magnus said.

"Are you here on your own?"

Magnus wasn't used to speaking into a microphone so he answered before the magician had time to hold it out. Mr. Bobbi asked him to repeat what he had said so everyone could hear. Magnus leaned toward the microphone.

"My friend's sitting over there."

Everyone looked at me again. I didn't know what to do, so I didn't do anything.

"So what's your friend going to say if I make you disappear?"

"I don't know," Magnus said.

As they were talking, Mr. Magic Bobbi reached one hand behind the red velvet curtain and pulled out a door on wheels with a big mirror on it. The mirror ended up right behind Magnus and the magician. The lights went out again, leaving just a spotlight shining on Magnus and Bobbi.

"Well, look at that!" the magician said. "You're already starting to disappear."

He turned and pointed at the mirror. Magnus turned as well. There was no sign of his reflection. The magician, the microphone, and everything else in the spotlight was visible. But not Magnus. The audience laughed and applauded. Magnus made a few little movements, but nothing showed in the mirror.

"I know," the magician said into the red microphone. "What if you try walking around it?"

He gestured to Magnus to take a look at the back, and Magnus walked around the mirror at the same time as the magician turned it the other way. Now Magnus's image appeared in the mirror. The magician spun the mirror again and showed it to all sides of the audience.

"OK, you can come out now," the magician said.

The audience applauded again. I saw Magnus try to say something, but because the magician had the microphone only his voice could be heard above the clapping and cheering of the audience.

"What a very vain fellow!" he said. "Sneaking inside the mirror like that. Well, it's time to come out now!"

Everyone laughed and clapped. I could see Magnus standing inside the mirror. He had his hands in his trouser pockets and was grinning sheepishly. I felt rather sorry for him then, standing there while everyone laughed.

It had always been easy to feel sorry for Magnus Gabrielsson. He never really fit in. We came from the same suburb, from similar families. Hardworking dads you never saw much of, mothers who took care of everything, wishing they were somewhere else. Comfortable enough to wish for something a bit better. No fancy holidays, but maybe a couple of weeks at a campsite in the vicinity of some moderately interesting attraction. Enough of an income to run one or even two secondhand cars, some smart clothes to show off in, and maybe even some basic improvements to the house. Enough for the kids to keep up with whatever was in fashion, more or less, or ignore it and spend all their pocket money on records and tapes instead.

We went to different schools but saw a lot of each other for a few years, drifting around the industrial park and the marsh behind it. He used to pick his nose, and he had a weird hairstyle as a teenager. He never talked much, kept himself to himself. There wasn't anything remarkable about him apart from the fact that he never belonged, never quite managed to figure out the things that mattered.

It felt odd sitting there watching him being mocked by the magician down in the ring. Everyone in the audience assumed that the subject of the trick was a grown man. Only I saw little Magnus Gabrielsson, who, when we were children, had sometimes wet himself when he got really scared.

4

The magician kept turning the mirror so that everyone could see it was completely flat. When he turned it in my direction it looked like Magnus was waving at me.

"Well, then," the magician said. "If you won't come out of your own accord, I'm going to have to take you backstage!"

He picked up the mirror frame with Magnus inside it, tucked it under his arm, and walked out. Everyone cheered and clapped. To my surprise I realized that I was laughing along with them.

The lights went up and the ringmaster reappeared.

"Mr. Magic Bobbiiii!" the ringmaster cried, and Bobbi ran back in to take the applause. There was no sign of Magnus.

After Bobbi, some acrobats came in on a little motorized cart. Because it was so small, they had to take turns riding on it. Hansen, or Larsen, came in and drove around on it as well.

The curtain closed and the rest of the lights went up. We had reached the intermission.

I sat for a while waiting for Magnus to come back as a

succession of rustling anoraks brushed past me to leave. When he didn't appear I headed to the little lobby to buy a drink from the vending machine.

There was quite a long line, and my fingers grew cold as I stood there waiting, even though it was almost June. I kept looking around to see if I could see Magnus. I thought I caught a glimpse of him behind a woman with curly hair and two children pulling in opposite directions. By the time they'd got out of the way he was gone again. Oh well, I thought. I'll see him when we go back to our seats again. I got my drink just as the band started to play. I hurried back to our seats along the uneven blue carpet with the strip of lights running alongside it.

The second half began with acrobats crawling in and out of various tunnels and holes, disappearing in one place only to reappear a moment later somewhere else entirely.

The audience was even more enthusiastic now, roaring with laughter at everything in the ring.

At one point one of the acrobats came very close to me. He was wearing a false mustache and glasses, but I could still see that it was Mr. Magic Bobbi behind the disguise. In fact, all the acrobats looked a lot like Mr. Magic Bobbi. I tried to work out how many of them there were and concluded that—purely theoretically—it would be possible for him to be playing all of them, if he moved fast enough between the holes and switched hats and mustaches when no one could see. When the act was over the ringmaster came back in, and it struck me that he looked a lot like Mr. Magic

Bobbi as well. On reflection, all the performers bore a striking resemblance to one another. Even the rather butch trapeze artist at the start.

I sat through the whole of the second act, waiting for Magnus. I had trouble concentrating on the circus. The finale was a sailor—definitely Mr. Magic Bobbi—singing "New York, New York" through the tinny red microphone. It was unbearable. But I still thought it was odd that Magnus hadn't come back. Didn't he want to see the other acts?

When the show was over and everyone left, I lingered to see if Magnus would appear among the benches. Perhaps he'd found something interesting at the back or had got talking to a member of the staff. Unless he'd got fed up and gone home? I stood around for a while, but eventually I started to feel silly so I left. On my way out I saw some security guards laughing. I couldn't help thinking they were laughing at me.

When I got home I kicked my shoes off so hard that they hit the wall. I screwed up the circus program and stuffed it in the bin, swore to myself, and went and lay on my bed with my clothes on.

I wasn't going to call Magnus Gabrielsson to ask where he'd got to. I thought it was very rude of him to disappear like that, especially when we'd arranged to go somewhere together. And it annoyed me that whenever we met I was always the one who ended up having to take care of him. Because that's exactly how it was. I always ended up helping Magnus Gabrielsson. The very first time we ever met I had to help him up, brush the leaves off him, and carry his ugly old rucksack all the way home.

5

I woke up early the next morning to the sound of rain pattering against the windows and the feeling that something wasn't right. I lay in bed for a while trying to remember if I'd had any strange dreams. Then I got up and phoned Magnus Gabrielsson. The line was busy. Which meant that at least he was home, I thought. But the same thing happened when I tried again an hour later, and an hour after that, so I started to wonder if it wasn't a bit odd after all. He couldn't still be on the phone, surely? Unless he'd left it off the hook?

I ate a bowl of muesli and thought about the previous day's visit to the circus. It was like trying to remember an unpleasant nightmare. Everything seemed just as peculiar today as it had the day before.

When I finished eating I put the bowl in the sink and went back into the bedroom to call Magnus again. I got the busy signal again, but when I tried once more the call didn't even connect. I stood in front of my records for a while, feeling stupid. I swapped Antony and the Johnsons and Joan As Police Woman around, then called Magnus's number again.

When there was still no answer I went out into the hall and put my shoes and coat on. I thought I might as well drop by Magnus's flat. It must have been ten years since I was last there.

I stepped out into the street and realized I should have taken an umbrella with me but couldn't be bothered to go back up and get one, so I pulled my hood up and kept close to the buildings in an attempt to stay out of the rain as best I could.

By the time I reached the door to Magnus's building I was soaked through, and realized that even if I had been able to remember the code to get in, they would have changed it by now. I stood beneath the porch, which barely sheltered me from the rain, peered through the glass, and saw the list of residents a little way inside the hall. I thought I could make out the name Gabrielsson shown as living on the first floor. I stepped back out into the rain and looked up. There was no sign of life on the first floor.

I stood there squinting through the rain until I felt the water slowly but surely soak through my jacket and sweater. I spotted a 7-Eleven a little way down the street and set off toward it at a run. There were a few plastic tables inside, as well as a counter and a couple of barstools from which you could get a good view of Magnus's building. I bought a cup of scalding hot tea and sat down. I shrugged off my jacket and hung it over the radiator beneath the table. I was the only person there apart from the cashier, and I considered taking my sweater off as well and sitting in my shirtsleeves but decided against it. I wiped myself down with some paper napkins. It didn't make much of a difference.

"They've turned the taps on full today," the cashier said, nodding toward my jacket.

I smiled. The cashier clattered about behind the counter. There was a badly tuned radio playing one of those Bryan Adams ballads whose titles I took a certain pride in not being able to identify. I tried to concentrate on Magnus's doorway, but the heavy rain was like a wall outside the window, which was getting more and more steamed up. After a while a figure appeared out of the rain. He rushed toward the shop door and shook himself like a wet dog when he came in. He looked at me, seeking an exchange of knowing glances about the terrible weather. I looked back toward Magnus's door again.

The cashier repeated the line about taps, and I wondered if he had only the one stock phrase.

A woman holding a newspaper over her head was heading straight toward the window, presumably to get as close to the building as possible. It struck me it was probably the first time I'd ever seen anyone do that with a newspaper in real life. It felt like a thing they'd do in—I don't know—France, say. Suddenly she was standing in front of me and we looked at each other. It felt a bit uncomfortable, realizing that we were so close to each other, with just the pane of glass between us. I thought about turning away, then remembered I was supposed to be keeping an eye on Magnus's door. I wasn't the one behaving oddly. She was.

We stayed like that for a moment, staring at each other, then I turned my attention back to Magnus's building again. The heavy door was swinging shut on the other side of the street and I realized what I had just caught a glimpse of: someone had gone in through the door.

I could have sworn it was Magnus.

6

I considered running over, but couldn't see any point. The door would still be closed. Whoever had gone inside would have vanished into the stairwell by the time I got there. I needed to keep a closer eye on people heading toward the building if I was to catch someone who could let me in. I stirred the hot tea with a plastic spoon.

The new customer came over to my table with his mug of coffee. He stopped so close that I realized he was going to say something to me. The moment he put his cup down on the table a light went on in one of the rooms on the first floor.

"Did it catch you by surprise?" the man beside me asked, nodding out at the rain.

I looked up at him, wondering what he meant. He gestured toward my wet clothes. I nodded and pointed at my jacket on the radiator under the table as I pondered asking if I could borrow the man's mobile to try Magnus again.

"Smart," the man with the coffee said.

"Yes," I said, and leaned over to feel my jacket. It had dried a little, and had a damp warmth, like clothes in a dryer before they're quite done. It felt nice now, but I knew it would be cold again the moment I put it on. When I sat back up the light in the flat had gone out.

"Dry?"

"No," I said, pulling the jacket on anyway before running out of the shop and over to the door.

I'd catch him on the way out.

It was still impossible to shelter under the porch of the building, and gusts of wind kept blowing fresh sheets of rain into my face. I huddled against the door as hard as I could.

No one came out, but after half an hour or so a woman appeared and let me in without any questions. She probably felt sorry for me when she saw how cold and wet I was, so I didn't need any of the excuses I'd been making up to help pass the time.

I squelched up the stairs and rang the doorbell. It sounded like someone was moving about inside the flat, but it was hard to tell because of the noise my wet clothes were making. A big puddle started to form around me. I tried to stand completely still and hold my breath so I could hear better, but there was no sound at all now. Maybe I'd imagined it. I nudged the letter box open.

"Magnus?" I called. "Is that you?"

It sounded stupid. The sort of thing someone would say in a film. So I didn't bother shouting again, and knocked instead. No answer.

After five minutes I walked slowly back down the stairs

and stopped in the entrance hall. It was still raining just as hard, and I decided to wait until the weather eased.

While I was standing there, leaning against the wall and looking out at the downpour through the glass, I caught sight of Jallo. He was walking along the other side of the street without a coat, and made a sudden dash across the road. Just before he reached the pavement it occurred to me that he might get a fright if he saw me standing perfectly still in the gloomy hall.

Sure enough he came to an abrupt halt when he caught sight of me. He screwed up his eyes and squinted as if he couldn't quite see if it really was me. He tapped on the glass and pointed at the door. I opened it for him.

"Bloody hell," he said, shaking off the worst of the water.

He looked at me as if he was expecting me to say something.

"What are you doing here?" he said.

I first met Jallo at a camp we attended each summer between the ages of thirteen and fifteen. He was a little older than me and went to Berg School: a hyperactive hippie kid who had moved from Finland with his mother a few years earlier. We spent a few summers together at that place—there were horses and a garden and you could paint, all that sort of thing. For a long time I thought we were in love with the same girl, but I don't remember us ever falling out about it. "People like us need to stick together," he had said. By that he was probably referring to the fact that we both liked synthesizer music, and it was important we stuck together because things weren't easy if you were into synth music back then. But I can't say I ever heard him play any music, and he knew surprisingly little about the subject when we talked about it. Then again, it was always difficult to get much of a handle on him. Admittedly he was older than me, but he seemed even older than his years. He got on well with grown-ups and was occasionally allowed to help the staff, and he was able to talk in that grown-up way that sometimes made it hard to say if he was one of us or one of them.

We only really started to spend more time together when we got to high school. After Dansson, he was the person I socialized with most—not that there was much competition. But I did genuinely enjoy his company.

"I thought I'd look in on Magnus," I said.

"Magnus?" Jallo said and sighed.

"Yes. What about you?"

"Oh, I don't know," he said with a shrug. "Do you want to do something?"

Despite having been friends for so long, Jallo often annoyed me. He spoke in a drawl that made me feel restless and irritated at the same time. His clothes looked as if he'd made them himself and he used to go on personal development courses in Holland, coming home with rosy cheeks talking about the more important things in life. It often felt like he lived in a different reality and that rules and regulations didn't apply to him the way they did to the rest of us. Everything seemed to be relative, conditional, as if it all could just as easily have been the other way around.

He never bore grudges. He was bound to have forgotten our row about "real friends" already. Nothing ever seemed to bother him. He just brushed himself off and carried on. He regarded every setback as an exciting challenge, and was only interested in how to move on from any given situation. He could turn on a sixpence and go off in completely the opposite direction without slowing down at all, as if it was the most natural thing in the world. Success didn't seem to affect him either. Everything was just "exciting" or "cool," and nothing was too insignificant not to warrant in-depth exploration. He could spend ages staring at you in silence, as if he was expecting something more. As if nothing was ever quite enough for him. As if there was always something he wanted to change.

Magnus didn't like Jallo. He said there was something weird about him. And of course there was. He always popped up just when you least expected it. He stood way too close. Didn't have any of the usual inhibitions. Always asked question after question, trying to get under your skin. It was as if no answer was ever good enough for him. It didn't matter what you said, he always followed up with another question.

"Why are you in such a hurry?"

"I don't want to be late."

"What for?"

"A class."

"Why not?"

"I don't want to miss the start."

"What difference would that make?"

"I'd get a black mark."

"Why would that matter?"

"It's not a good idea to get black marks."

"Why not?"

"Leave off!"

Whenever you said something, he would nod, and you'd assume you'd reached some sort of agreement. Then he'd make a completely different decision instead. Maybe he was just shy or being polite, but it always made me feel a bit stupid. As if he always knew more than me in any given situation.

Before he even graduated from high school he had developed an entrepreneurial spirit. He registered as self-employed and set up a phone line for people who "wanted to get things off their chest."

"This is the future," he told me. "The service sector! The soft economy, human issues. Contact, interaction, interpersonal values. Industry," he said with a snort. "Industry is so over, you know. There's no future in *stuff*. No one wants more *stuff*. What society needs now is someone to take care of all the lost souls industry has left behind. You need to take care of your brand, construct your own style, your own way of dealing with other people, understanding and appreciating them. That's the future. Communication. You're home and dry if you know how to communicate. But if you don't, then . . ."

Over the next few years self-employment became a private company, and the private company became a public limited company. These days he was renting office space to run some sort of clinic, as well as various other questionable activities. He had customers he called clients, but not so many that you couldn't show up there pretty much whenever you felt like to drink coffee and talk rubbish while Jallo proudly showed off his latest purchases, notwithstanding his proclamations against "stuff."

"Take a look at this! Velvet!" he said, patting a couch he'd placed in the middle of the room.

He had furnished the room with heavy red curtains, hand-woven rugs, and big, annoying, garish pictures that didn't seem to be of anything much, but which he was still very proud of. He always said the way things looked was vital.

"It's more important than you'd think," he said. "People often pass judgment at first sight."

I don't know what he did to the poor fools who went to see him, but they must have been happy since they kept going back.

* * *

He had long hair, sometimes loose, sometimes in a ponytail. If you saw him out in the street you could easily think he was a dropout, a "resting" rock musician or some other unemployed hedonist who had been taking a few too many drugs, whereas he actually ran that clinic as well as a number of other businesses. He'd just applied to register a new form of therapy and was, if you believed what he said, "on his way to becoming a real player." If he was on his way to an important meeting you might see him with a suit hanging off his lanky frame. But it was as if he didn't care what other people thought when it came down to it. He did exactly what he liked, when he liked.

He was perfectly capable of talking crap about Magnus, for instance.

"Forget him," he might say before dragging you off somewhere, even though you'd made other arrangements. As if what you were doing really didn't matter, and whatever new thing he had going on was bound to be way more interesting.

I told Jallo that Magnus wasn't home but there was something strange going on, seeing as I had heard noises inside the flat. And his phone was engaged the whole time. Jallo listened and nodded. I told him how I'd seen the lights go on and off. In the end we both went back upstairs and knocked on the door. No answer.

"So he's not home," Jallo said.

"What d'you mean?" I said.

"If he was home he'd open the door."

I looked at him and he looked back at me. As if it was as simple as that.

I told him that Magnus and I had been to the circus and I hadn't seen him since.

"OK," Jallo said, nodding. "So?"

I looked at him.

"So I thought I'd try to get hold of him," I said.

Jallo tilted his head a few times with an expression that could be taken to mean that he'd been hoping we could do something more entertaining.

"Why don't you write a letter?" Jallo asked.

"To Magnus?"

"Yes," Jallo said.

I sighed.

"You know what I think you should do?" he said after a pause, brightening up as if he'd just had an idea. "I think you should check out this place."

Jallo found an old till receipt in one pocket and a pen in the other. He scribbled something on the scrap of paper and handed it to me. I took it. He stuck his tongue out and caught a raindrop that was trickling from his wet hair. Then he stiffened and raised his eyebrows. He pulled something from the pocket of his hoodie and held it up triumphantly.

"Toffee," he said.

I glanced at my watch while Jallo unwrapped the toffee

with his long, thin fingers and put it in his mouth. He smacked his lips as he sucked it, still looking at me. As if it was down to the pair of us now. As if I had to decide what we should do.

"Bought any records lately?" he asked as he chewed the toffee.

"Yep," I said.

"'Sail Away' by Enya is pretty good," he said.

I didn't respond to that.

We stood like that for a while, and the only thing that happened was that the toffee in his mouth got smaller, and the obscene slurping sounds came faster and faster. Every so often he held up his hand and looked at it. It looked chapped and red.

"I've started getting dry skin again," he said. "Need to remember to wear gloves."

Eventually I realized I had no choice but to leave. Jallo stood where he was, still looking at me in that forlorn way, and I thought it was just as well to get going before he asked if he could come with me. I pushed the front door open and felt the relentless rain on my face. I held up the receipt Jallo had given me. It came from the Gryningen health food shop on Folkungagatan. Jallo's handwriting was as bad as a doctor's, and the rain was already washing some of it away. But I could just about make out the address: Bondegatan 3A.

I stood there awhile, shuffling from one foot to the other. Then I went home.

7

Bondegatan 3A? What was that supposed to mean? I didn't like the way Jallo went about things. He always saw so many different ways of approaching a subject, the possibilities seemed endless. If you lost your wallet, for instance, and the police couldn't help you, why not try hypnosis? Or a Facebook group? Everything seemed equally valid to him.

He would muddle brand-new research findings from the Karolinska Hospital with long-forgotten medieval remedies. Grumble that a lot of conventional psychology was too rigid.

For a while he tried to cultivate oyster mushrooms in a garage on Kungsholmen. He had a load of cardboard boxes that looked like little red cottages lined up along the wall behind the cars.

"Low rent," he said. "Decent margins."

I don't know what happened, if it just wasn't profitable after all, or if there was some sort of problem with the garage or people driving over the boxes. But he seemed to have put the project on hold, anyway. It had been a long time since he had mentioned anything about the "mush-room industry."

More recently he had embarked upon a proper psychology course.

"Having a bit of paper that says you can do stuff seems to be so important," he said.

I agreed that it might not be a bad idea to acquire a bit more evidence-based knowledge if you were serious about setting yourself up in that line of business. So he had applied, been accepted, and decided to study enough course units at the university to get himself a certificate, but it was highly doubtful that he'd stick at it for long enough.

"Takes a hell of a long time," he said.

Predictably, his studies ended up taking a back seat in favor of his other activities. Being "certified" no longer seemed so important, as Jallo put it, with air quotes. People would still come to his clinic.

The last time I was there he showed me a karaoke machine. He said he'd got it to help his clients "lower their guard."

"The atmosphere can get a bit too tense," he said, looking through the songs on offer. "And of course it's pretty cool, too!"

Maybe he used rocks or crystals, or did some sort of CBT treatment? I don't really know what he offered his clients. Apart from karaoke, of course.

It was impossible to get any real grip on all his plans and

activities. Maybe even he didn't know. He seemed to collect slightly dodgy people and together they would come up with unconventional ways to earn money. His ideas often seemed to involve telesales.

Bondegatan 3A. There could be anything there. But perhaps it would be silly not to make use of his contacts, I reasoned. Whoever they might be.

8

That evening Magnus's phone was still busy. I called five times and never got through. I watched some TV, had a cup of tea, then went around the flat turning the lights out before I went to bed. I knew I should get to sleep just after eleven in order to be vaguely awake for work early the next morning. There was nothing good on after the late news anyway. The programs would only get worse and worse until eventually I was left watching repeats of *The Fall Guy* from the early 1980s or staring at the rolling news on TV Vision. Even so, I still found myself sitting on the sofa with the phone in my hand. Why was the line still busy? Did he have that many friends to talk to? Or had he pulled his phone out of the socket? Why hadn't he called me? I put the phone down next to me on the sofa and listened to the busy signal for a while before I pressed the red button.

Sure enough, SVT was showing a documentary about a school orchestra tour, Channel 5 had an American poker program, TV3 a reality program in which the participants pretended to be friends before voting each other out in the hope of becoming the World's Biggest Loser. By the time *The*

Fall Guy finished it was two o'clock. I picked up the phone. Looked at it. It rang. I answered at once.

No one said anything, there was just a faint hum, but I could hear someone breathing on the other end. I switched the television off, and the flat plunged into darkness. And complete silence. I stood up and walked over to the window.

"Hello?" I said.

Still no response, but I sensed someone there. I tried to breathe as quietly as possible even though I could hear my heart beating faster and faster.

"Hello?" I said once more. "Who am I talking to?"

Not that there's anyone talking back, I thought, listening to the silence on the line. Down in the street a billboard advertising men's underwear was lit up, casting a faint streak of light across the building opposite, where all the lights were out. I pressed the phone closer to my ear and tried to imagine the person at the other end. The silent caller. It felt decidedly unsettling.

"Is that Magnus?" I said after a while.

There was a noise—it sounded like fabric or possibly a hand. Unless it was just static on the line. It was impossible to tell. I stood perfectly still in my pitch-black living room, feeling the warmth of the phone against my cheek.

"What . . . Is that you, Magnus?" I repeated. "Is everything OK?"

When there was no answer to that either, I decided to

stay quiet as well. I walked slowly back and forth in the darkened room, waiting. It felt like the two of us, the caller and I, were each waiting for the other. I stood for a long time leaning against the frame of the kitchen door. I rested my head gently against the wood and heard a slight tap as the phone knocked the frame. I angled it away from my mouth.

I ended up in the hall, in front of the mirror. Because the flat was in total darkness I couldn't see anything in the mirror. There was nothing for it to reflect. I wondered for a moment if you could say I was in the mirror even though I couldn't see myself. I pressed the phone to my ear and because neither of us was speaking it was almost as if I was listening to myself. I got the sense that the silence was somehow betraying how anxious I was and did my best not to breathe into the receiver too much. It wasn't nice, listening to your own anxiety.

"Where's Magnus?" I said.

I imagined I could hear that the breathing at the other end was just as nervous. As if there was something stressful, discomforting about the whole situation. As if he or she had been about to say something but had thought better of it. Perhaps they were frightened and didn't dare speak?

In the end there was a click and I realized that the other person had hung up. I paced the flat for a while. I switched the bedside light on and sat on the bed staring at the phone. If it was him, why hadn't Magnus said anything? And if it wasn't him, who was it? Could there have been something wrong with the microphone on his phone? That sort of thing sometimes happened. No, because I could clearly hear someone breathing. So why hadn't he said anything? Was he afraid to?

I lay back and opened the IKEA catalogue on my chest, but the usual undemanding joy of idle browsing wasn't there. After ten minutes I got up and dialed the same number again. No answer.

Being awake at night can have its advantages. As long as you can manage to suppress all thoughts of sleep and the tiredness you're bound to feel the next day. The night offers a stillness, a concentration that can make you think you've found a gap in time.

I put my headphones on and listened to Prefab Sprout's *Jordan: The Comeback*. I clicked to get to "Moon Dog" and sat in the armchair next to the stereo listening to the intro, which always calmed me down and made me feel I was going somewhere. Even if that just meant onward through the night. Somehow I managed to fall asleep like that.

10

I hate it when people disappear inside mirrors and don't come back. It's a real pain. You just don't do that sort of thing. But if people still insist on doing it they usually come back sooner or later, and you find out what happened. Then you both sit and laugh about how gullible you were, and at the entertaining but slightly humiliating fact that you fell for such a simple trick. But if they disappear and don't come back, then in my opinion the joke stops being funny. It makes you question the way you see the world, and I really don't like doing that. I'd be perfectly happy to keep hold of the way I see the world right now, with a tolerably good understanding of how things work. I'd prefer to keep hold of my friends and be able to trust my senses.

I worked behind the bakery counter of the NK depart-ment store. I would stand there wrapping bread and pastries, literally imprisoned in a glass cage under the gaze of the customers, all of whom had just one and the same wish: that as soon as I was done serving another customer, I would press the button so that their number would finally come up on the ticketed queuing system. If I took too long someone would call out, "Young man, what do you think you're here for?"

The boss had told us we should just smile if that happened.

All things considered it was a good, reliable job. I mean, people are always going to want bread, and they're always going to want to buy it from NK. I was fairly happy there and did the job well enough. But I was due to start at nine o'clock on Monday morning, and when I woke up in my armchair it was already quarter to. I got up and pulled my headphones off, and it was only when the noise disappeared that I realized I had slept all night with last night's music in my ears. It echoed in my head as I brushed my teeth and pulled on my shoes and coat.

I arrived at work at half past nine and got some pointed stares from the girls who had had to cover for me. Fortunately the boss was nowhere in sight, so I clicked to the button for the next customer and tried to compensate for my late arrival by smiling even more than usual. By lunchtime it felt as if that smile had eaten its way into my features and become a grimace that was more frightening than welcoming.

I tried calling Magnus twice from work, but there was no answer. No answering-machine message. Nothing.

As the day went on, the trays from the bakery emptied, and they had to be cleaned before they were returned. I usually tried to get that job, which meant twenty minutes or half an hour at the sink in the back. Without an audience. After lunch I hauled all the trays into the kitchen and turned the tap on. I pulled off the fake bow tie that was part of the bakery-counter uniform. The girls had to wear frilly aprons and have their hair up. I had the male equivalent: a shirt with a bow tie on an elastic band that pinched your throat. It was fixed to the top button, and would snap off when you unfastened it. I stood there staring into space for a while. What on earth was going on? Magnus had gone missing, and now someone I didn't know was calling me in the middle of the night and not saying a word.

* * *

The more I thought about it, the more I felt sure that the silence on the line was in some nebulous but undeniable sense—a bit like the way Lou Reed is connected to David Bowie, or Jonas Bonetta to Josh Garrels—connected to Propaganda's third single, "p:Machinery."

12

There was no good reason for "p:Machinery" by Propaganda to pop into my head. Even so, I listened to the whole of their *A Secret Wish* album when I got home, trying to figure out what it was about the silence on the phone line that had made me think of Propaganda. Sure, that was the sort of music we listened to most, me and Magnus. But what was it about that particular track? The computerized bleeps at the start, or just the dark, foreboding atmosphere? Listening to it again didn't help. When I was putting the record back I wasn't sure if it ought to move along a few places, closer to China Crisis and Heaven 17, who admittedly had more of an acoustic sound but still belonged to that same part of the synth music scene.

That evening I swapped the Pixies and the Ramones, which meant that there was no room for the Sex Pistols and Andy Hull's solo album, so they had to be squeezed in on the shelf below, which didn't feel great, seeing as that was the shelf I had been happiest with up until then. I stood there for a while wondering if that meant I couldn't buy any more albums in that subgenre, or if I would just have to expand it instead. There wasn't room on the wall for any more shelves. Maybe I'd have to sell some records or use those plastic sleeves. I didn't want to put my records in plastic sleeves. It felt tacky. Disrespectful. As if all records could be reduced to a flat disc with no spine. Besides, it ruined the whole idea of a record collection if you couldn't see which records were lined up next to each other. In that case I might as well give up and switch to Spotify, I reasoned, and end up left with everything and nothing. An undefined mass of tracks on a computer where you could sneak a listen to individual tracks without any sense of the integrity of the album and the culture of album sleeves. No structure.

That was pretty much how people used to listen to the *Chart Show* at school. Listening idly and never learning names and album titles. Never knowing where the different tracks belonged. As if music was just one big river, something you couldn't influence, like fog, or pollution.

There were two schools in the area where Magnus and I grew up. One good, one not so good. Berg School and Vira Elementary.

Berg School was notorious for its thugs, bullies, and genuinely criminal students. It was widely regarded as a "bad school." A big, old-fashioned slum school where kids ended up if their families lived in the wrong place or didn't have the right sort of influence, the right contacts in the council, didn't have the energy to keep nagging and writing letters to the education office. A place for kids with no ambitions.

The more fortunate of us went to Vira Elementary School. A modern school in nice buildings that had a "salad bar" and flower beds on the grounds and guaranteed good grades. Those of us who went to Vira didn't socialize with the kids who went to Berg. We were told—by teachers, other pupils, and not least of all our parents—that they were all either illiterate, hooligans, or drug addicts. The papers had written about the "situation" at Berg School, where violence and threatening behavior were part of daily life. Our headmaster appeared on local television, tilting his head thoughtfully and lamenting the way things had developed at Berg while simultaneously declaring that there was no bullying at Vira Elementary.

Vira only had well-behaved pupils who were motivated to study. Our headmaster said that at our school we helped each other and put all our efforts into our studies. And if there was ever any bullying, he crowed on that television program, the bullies would have him to answer to.

I always imagined life at Berg School like a prison film, where different gangs were in charge, doling out punishments and demanding bribes and protection money.

Panic broke out when there was talk of transferring some of us from Vira to Berg School. The intake had been too big and the classes were too large. Unless this was just an attempt by the council to mix up the socioeconomic groups a little in order to reduce segregation and create a more equal society. Vira was considerably smaller, and in order to make space some of us might have to be moved to Berg School.

The parents, led by Dennis's dad and Mia Lindström's mum, attended a crisis meeting with the headmasters and representatives of the council. Rumor had it that Dennis's dad had torn a strip off the people from the council and told them they were incompetent and how he'd see to it that they lost their jobs and never got another position with any authority. Anna Hamberg's mum said that if her daughter was going to be transferred to Berg School, they may as well put her in a young offenders' institution there and then. Several of them, parents and teachers alike, wept openly. In the end nothing came of the whole thing. Our parents were able to draw a collective sigh of relief, content in the knowledge that we could carry on going to the very best of schools.

I didn't know anything about Berg School apart from what Magnus and Jallo told me and the rumors that used to do the rounds. I was just immensely grateful that I didn't have to go there, because I was a "special" child, as my teacher put it. The sort who can find the social side of things a bit difficult, as he told my parents.

"And obviously that's a bit of a challenge for the rest of the class," he said.

I didn't say anything. I rarely did in those days. I did what I usually did. Waited until it was over so I could put my headphones on again. I learned at an early age that most things only got worse the more you talked. After a lot of nagging and sulking I had finally got myself a Walkman, partly paid for by my parents, and spent almost all my free time making mix tapes that I wandered about listening to. The best part of the day was in between lessons when I could put my headphones on and disappear into my own soundtrack, drifting along listening to one song after the other and seeing the world more as a sequence of moving images set to music.

At Vira Elementary there were two musical genres you could choose between. You either liked synth music or hard rock. There was nothing in between. We'd heard of people who listened to reggae, and older people who listened to all sorts of things, jazz, for instance, but the choice at school was simple: synthesizers or hard rock. If you didn't make the choice for yourself, someone else would do it for you. If you weren't into rock, you were automatically a synth fan.

The hard-rock kids were the overwhelming majority, but that was just as much to do with the whole image as the music. Torn jeans and studded belts, long blond curly hair or dead straight black hair. Armbands with skulls on them, that sort of thing. Some of them wore battered leather boots and shark-tooth necklaces, but they were still pretty tame compared to the rockers from Berg School you used to run into down at the shopping center. They had tattoos, carried ghetto blasters on their shoulders, and knew people who were real punks. At Vira all you needed to be a rocker was an Iron Maiden T-shirt. Dennis had permed hair and usually wore a clean, unblemished tennis shirt, but every so often he would wear a leather bracelet to discreetly indicate which group he belonged to. He talked a lot about W.A.S.P., chainsaws, Twisted Sister, and women being crucified onstage. Synth-pop was a term of abuse.

In our class we muddled along well enough, but there was a definite hierarchy, with Dennis at the top and the rest of us in descending order, with me close to, if not right at, the bottom. It didn't bother me. It wasn't something that was ever spoken about. That was just how it was. And it somehow made a lot of sense, everyone having clearly defined roles. There was never any need for fighting or threatening behavior. Things sorted themselves out of their own accord, with glances and whispers and the number of chairs between me and the others in the cafeteria. I was always aware of the situation and stuck to the rules as well as I could.

Most of the time I wasn't bothered by it. I had my music. As soon as I put my headphones on they could push me about however they wanted without it mattering at all. Sometimes they stood on my heels so my shoes would come off, but it wasn't exactly hard to put them back on again. Sometimes I was just unlucky. Like the time a note with a vulgar—extremely vulgar—sentence on it ended up on my desk, and Eva, our English teacher, spotted it. I wasn't sure I understood all the words, and certainly not what they meant, but because the note contained Eva's name I was summoned to see the headmaster.

The same thing happened in Year 9 when they composed a fake "love letter" in my name to Maddy, which she showed to her teacher, who brought it to the attention of the headmaster because of the coarse language and threatening, chauvinistic tone. The headmaster said it was deeply insulting to women, and I would have to apologize to Maddy in person. He also said that if I wanted to have any contact with the opposite sex in the future, I would have to learn that that sort of language simply wasn't acceptable. It was far too much bother to try to explain what had happened, so I did as they said and apologized. That seemed the simplest solution, and it was all over fairly quickly. A few short platitudes by Maddy's locker, then I could put my headphones back on and retreat into the world of music again.

The times I ended up battered and bruised, or my schoolbooks got ruined, were almost always the result of a prank or an accident. Like the time I came out of the shower after PE and all my clothes were gone, and I had to cover myself with paper towels all the way to the headmaster's office, where they let me borrow some clothes from the lost and found. That was probably my fault. Maybe I hadn't heard something because I had my headphones on? That happened quite a lot. Things usually got sorted out after I got told off or had to go and see the headmaster. It was just how things had always been for me.

Once I'd slotted Lotte Lenya and Ute Lemper back in next to Kurt Weill again I was left standing there with an old Madness album in one hand and a Starsailor single from 2003 in the other. Still no solution to the Sex Pistols and Andy Hull dilemma. I pondered the possibility of getting rid of some records and wondered where to draw the line. That Starsailor single, for instance: it was pretty good in its own way, even if I never played it. I was reading the back of the sleeve to see if it featured any names I recognized when the phone rang. I picked it up.

"Hello?" I said.

There was obviously someone there.

"Hello?" I tried again, a bit louder this time.

Still silence.

I turned the stereo down and walked over to the window, making up my mind to wait. Several minutes of silence followed. I pressed the phone closer to my ear to see if I could hear any sounds in the background that might give me an idea of where the person was, but there was nothing. After a while I went on leafing through my records and almost managed to forget there was someone at the other end of the line.

I pulled out my records and laid them in piles. It started

to feel almost natural to have that sort of mute company in my ear. Whoever it was, we had now spent a while in each other's company, and if it was Magnus I wasn't going to do him the favor of making any more stupid pleas. There was a good chance he'd burst into laughter and make me feel ridiculous. I wasn't going to give him that pleasure. If he wanted to play at not speaking, he was welcome to. I was just going to carry on as usual.

"Silence is easy," I heard myself say in English.

I looked down at the Starsailor single and saw that that was the title of the song. There was complete silence at the other end of the line, but I reasoned that I might as well say that as nothing at all. So I put "Weird Fishes" by Radiohead into the CD player and turned the volume up. I held the phone up to the speaker. When the song came to an end I clicked to end the call.

13

The next day I called my friend Dansson. It was a perfectly ordinary phone call, where both people talk, sometimes interrupt each other, agree on something, neither person just disappears, you say goodbye, and hang up. You don't make the call and then not speak. No mysterious silence, no weird musical excursions. A perfectly normal phone call.

We agreed to meet up in Record King after work.

Because I was the only guy on the bakery counter and people prefer to be served by pretty girls, I always got the sense that people felt they had drawn the short straw when they ended up with me. Especially older men. Sometimes women got it into their heads that they were going to have to teach me a thing or two, or at least check if I knew the names of the different loaves and what spices they contained. Every so often people would tilt their heads and patronize me. But occasionally someone would ask to speak to me because they assumed I was the girls' boss. I'm not sure which was more embarrassing.

That day people kept buying bread and pastries, and I took orders for five identical student-graduation cakes.

"You see," a man in late middle age said to me after telling me to fetch a pen and paper, "I was thinking of something a bit special, if you follow?"

I assured him that I understood.

"I thought it would be nice if the cake looked like a graduation cap, if you get what I mean?"

I nodded and he gave me a knowing smile.

"A traditional princess cake, but with white icing instead of green, and with a black ribbon around it. And I thought it might be possible to give it a little peak on one side. Do you understand what I mean?"

I nodded once more. Evidently that wasn't enough.

"The cake *is* a student graduation cap. Do you see?"

14

Record King was located in a basement at the bottom of a short flight of steps. The building had a lot of potential. The little sunlight that penetrated the dusty windows up by the ceiling served mostly to bleach the pale yellow vinyl records lined up as a vague sort of display, but really they just declared: we've given up.

Dansson and I were regulars there, but these days I couldn't help feeling a bit uncomfortable as I browsed through what was probably the weakest aspect of the whole enterprise: the stock. The same old records in the same places they had been the year before and the year before that, and where they had perhaps always been, in dusty rows in the homemade racks the Record King himself had constructed sometime in the early 1980s.

Dansson was already standing over by the vinyl when I arrived. He looked up and nodded to me when the doorbell rang. I went down the steps and walked over to him to stand the way we usually stood, lost in covers and track lists.

* * *

Dansson was actually named Dan Hansson, but everyone had called him Dansson since high school or national service or whenever it was that someone was hungover enough to come up with the ingenious idea of combining his first and last names and ending up with Dansson.

I didn't know how many people called him Dansson, but that's what he said the first time we met: "Call me Dansson—everyone does." It was just after we'd tossed a coin for a Human League single. He won and probably still felt a bit guilty about it.

We used to stand opposite each other in Record King, flicking through the racks back in the days when new stock would arrive each week. Back when there was always a line of expectant teenagers wanting to listen to twelve-inch singles and albums on the record player on the counter. Back when there was still a three-minute limit to trials and Dansson and I would listen together. Now you could listen as long as you wanted. The way I saw it, they were just happy to have anyone who wanted to listen to anything at all. I'd never met up with Dansson much outside Record King, except a few times at concerts or in clubs. Who knows, maybe I was the only person who ever called him Dansson? I'd never met any of his friends. I might even be Dansson's only friend.

He had a particular ability to tell a story, and then tell it again with a few minor adjustments, which gave the impression that he was constantly tweaking the truth. Sometimes he said the same thing a third time, usually recounting what had happened to people he knew, things they had done or tried, pop and rock stars and celebrities and inventors they had met. I often got the feeling that if they weren't actually imaginary friends, they were certainly exaggerated versions of real people. Possibly people he'd read or heard about. Unless he just made everything up on the spur of the moment? It didn't really make any difference. I'd stopped paying much attention by then. I just used to mumble and nod as we wandered around looking at records.

I pulled out a Simple Minds double album that I must have looked at and decided not to buy at least a dozen times before. I turned it over, then put it back again.

"All right?" Dansson asked after a while.

"Yeah," I said.

I saw that Rufus Wainwright's *Want One* was among the new arrivals, even though it had been out several years. I thought about buying it for the final track, "Dinner at Eight," but decided it was too expensive.

The doorbell rang and the Record King himself came down the steps with a microwave meal and a small carton of juice in a transparent plastic bag. He said hello and disappeared into the little room behind the counter. We could steal anything we wanted in here, I thought. But which of all these records would either of us actually want to steal?

"He's DJing in the Bar the day after tomorrow," Dansson said, nodding toward the back room.

"Oh," I said.

"Are you going?"

"Not sure," I said.

Dansson was examining a Prince picture disc. He ran his finger gently across the vinyl to feel if it was scratched.

"Do you remember Magnus Gabrielsson?" I said after a while.

"Roxette?" Dansson said.

"Yes, that's him."

A memory flashed through my head. On one occasion in Dansson's company I happened to demonstrate a surprisingly comprehensive knowledge of Roxette, which had left him staring at me open-mouthed. He demanded an explanation. I had to confess to having spent a number of hours in the company of Roxette. But I explained that it had been a very long time ago, and it was all Magnus Gabrielsson's fault. Which meant I had to tell him all about Magnus Gabrielsson.

15

When I was in high school I always used to wait outside the classroom for two or three tracks so I could go to my locker in peace and quiet, after most of the others had gone. Then I would pack my things together and walk down toward the shopping center, still with music in my ears.

There, for a brief period each afternoon, the kids from both schools merged to form a sea of children, which quickly overflowed past the bus station and newsagent and spread across the neighborhood. As if someone had poured a bucket of kids onto the streets, which ran in and out of the shops and across the squares, kicking bins and lampposts and anything else that wasn't tied down, until a last trickle dispersed on the outskirts of the community. It was nice to be a bit behind everyone else. Even if it was impossible not to bump into someone from Berg School. They seemed to belong to a different species. Bigger, rougher, noisier.

Among them was one guy who didn't seem to belong. Who always kept out of the way. I always expected them to shove and hit him, but that never happened. Quite the opposite, in fact. They all avoided him. It was as if he smelled. Of loneliness and isolation. No one wanted to get too close to that. Often he was just standing at the street corner by the post office. It was hard to see why. It was like he'd been dumped there. Left behind, abandoned. Like he was waiting for his mum to come and pick him up. Rescue him from this strange world. As if his whole life was just a mistake. A parenthesis.

But no one ever came.

I don't remember the first time I noticed him. He was just there. As if he'd always been there. Like part of the furniture. You got used to him. He was often left standing by the post office, waiting, looking at his digital watch.

When he eventually started to move I noticed he was walking the same way as me. Walking without any expression at all on his face. Nothing about him stood out. He probably thought he was invisible, but in actual fact it was impossible not to notice his thin figure sliding along the facades of the buildings, backing away to make sure he didn't get too close to anyone. Sometimes he and I were the only people around, but he still stayed at a safe distance of at least ten meters from me. When we emerged from the shopping center and I set off along the path, he often walked a little way into the forest and tried to keep out of the way by deploying a number of tactics that were impossible not to notice. As if he wanted to emphasize the fact that he didn't belong. At first I just felt sorry for him and assumed he wasn't all there. But as time passed it started to feel more like self-imposed exclusion. Something he was almost proud of, and clung to with irritating meticulousness. He never looked up, never spoke to anyone. Just kept looking at his watch almost obsessively, as if he was hoping we were about to enter a different time. That this would all be over, in the past. Long ago. He never showed any emotion and kept his distance with impressive persistence. As if the rest of us could never catch him. Even if we'd wanted to.

For several weeks we carried on like that, skirting around each other. After a while I began to wonder if he had started waiting for me. It felt almost as if he was trying to attract my attention with his weird way of keeping to himself. I wondered if he was hanging about by the post office simply so he could set off at the same time as me. Hiding and making a big deal of it. As soon as we reached the path he would always walk parallel to me in among the trees. Even if he never looked in my direction, it was as if he was constantly keeping an eye on me with that expression of self-proclaimed inferiority and idiocy. Big eyes, mouth open. Rucksack slung over both shoulders. Nobody normal ever used more than one strap.

One day I stopped and looked straight at him with Alphaville's "Forever Young" in my ears. He stopped too. Red-cheeked. Runny nose. He wiped his nose on his coat sleeve. Everyone else had already gone off ahead of us. He and I were the only ones left on the path leading to the blocks of flats. I don't know what he was thinking. Perhaps this was the moment he'd been waiting for. Perhaps he wanted me to make contact? Either way, he didn't do anything at all. Just stood there staring stupidly at me. In the end I stuck my middle finger up at him. I don't know why I did that. I'd probably just had enough. Unless I wanted to show him which of us was in charge. He stuck his finger up back at me and I don't know why that annoyed me so much. Maybe I was just surprised that he had the nerve to do it. Perhaps I thought it was childish, unimaginative, unless I was just confident that I could deal with him—that he was playing with fire. What on earth was he thinking? Without realizing what I was doing, I jumped across the ditch, ran over to him, and shoved him hard in the chest, knocking him to the ground.

It was so easy. No sooner had my hands struck his thin frame than he tumbled back, his woolly hat falling off. He didn't make any attempt to defend himself. Just tumbled into the undergrowth with a look of surprise. I regretted what I'd done at once and crouched down to see if he was OK.

"What the hell . . . ," he muttered.

"Just take it easy," I said, pulling my headphones off. "Are you hurt?"

"Oh, not too badly," he said as he sat up and rolled his head about as if to check he hadn't injured his neck. As if he was used to it. It felt like he knew exactly what to do after that sort of attack.

"What did you do that for?" he said.

I shook my head and mumbled an apology.

I helped him to his feet and brushed the leaves off him, the way I'd seen adults do with other kids. I picked up his rucksack and carried it for him as we set off along the path again, side by side.

"Do you like synth music or hard rock?" I asked after a while.

"I don't know," he said.

"That means you like synth music," I said.

He nodded, and after that we didn't say much. He kept quiet, and I had my headphones on. In the end I started to talk about the music I was listening to. I explained the running order. Why they'd been arranged like that. The thinking behind it. He nodded and seemed to want to hear more. I told him about the different groups, how they fitted together, what the differences were between them, and who did what. I described the splits in different bands, who had been in them and how they had changed over time.

We ended up walking together most days. I would pick him up outside the post office, then we would walk out of the shopping center together. When we got to the path we usually branched off and went in among the trees instead.

I explained that the difference between synth music and hard rock was mostly about attitude, a feeling that could be difficult to describe to the uninitiated. I explained, for instance, that someone who liked synth music could pretty much listen to any sort of music, as long as it wasn't metal. It just had to have a synthy feel to it.

"You have to steer clear of monsters and crucified women and chainsaws . . . stuff like that. Definitely no chainsaws. Not too much guitar distortion. But ordinary guitars are no problem. A lot of people are needlessly frightened of guitars."

"They are?" Magnus said.

I nodded.

"There are quite a lot of guitars even in synth music," I explained.

"Are there?"

"Sure, just think of groups like Spandau Ballet or Duran Duran. They use a lot of guitars."

I gave him a few moments to absorb this information. Perhaps he'd never thought of them as synth groups until now. Perhaps he didn't even know who they were. He was clearly a novice and needed to be educated.

"Just from the way they look, some groups can be difficult to distinguish from hard-rock groups," I went on. "Dead or Alive, for instance. I know a lot of people who wonder about them."

I didn't know any, but I'd been a bit unsure myself at first.

"You have to look at the details," I continued. "Then when you listen to them it's obvious, of course."

I played one track after another to illustrate the differences.

Sometimes he had to hear a song several times before he understood properly. He nodded and smiled when he realized what I meant. I used the Cure to explain the direct connection between synth music and miserablist rock, which was nothing to do with hard rock. Magnus soaked up the information like a sponge. After a while he began to ask intelligent follow-up questions, and I could see he was keeping up. He seemed genuinely interested. The lost kid outside the post office had turned into a true connoisseur, thanks to my musical instruction. He was learning to tell the difference between fakes and originals, one-hit wonders from artists with real staying power. The good thing about Magnus was that he was such a quick learner. You never had to browbeat him or explain things too many times. I thought he was an excellent pupil.

Magnus went to Berg School. But probably not all that regularly. I didn't know anything about the state of his education, but he always showed up, whether or not we'd arranged to meet. I got the feeling that he was neglecting his schoolwork in order to hang out with me. Who knows—maybe he'd stopped going to school altogether?

Besides listening to music we used to run around the patch of land behind the industrial park where the spring meltwater made its way down to the marsh. We wandered about in the big, tranquil forest with its tall firs and deep moss in almost perpetual motion. We slid down rocks and clambered up slopes covered with slippery grass, low branches scratching our faces.

The marsh was treacherous. Everyone knew that. According to local legend, there was quicksand beneath it that would suck everything down into it. Some of the businesses in the industrial park, which seemed to change hands regularly, were obviously dumping their rubbish there. There were all sorts of things—empty oil drums, tins, old crates, rags, scraps of metal, lamps and cables, all squelching among the branches and mounds of grass, which stuck up like islands from the brown sludge. In the middle of a clearing, on top of a pile of leaves, or what had once been leaves—half leaves, half soil—there was a big velour armchair that oozed water if you pressed it. With each passing day the garbage would sink a little deeper into the marsh, and after a while it swallowed everything. Its appetite seemed insatiable. By the edge of the marsh we found some sodden pages torn from porn magazines, which we hung to dry in the trees and tried to put back together. The water had stuck some of the pages together, making them impossible to pry apart no matter how hard we tried. But we spent most of our time down there just wandering around, kicking the rubbish sticking out of the water and trying not to get our feet wet, passing the time by talking about all manner of things.

We used to race each other, commenting on our performance like sports presenters. It was always more of a game than a real competition. Not like PE classes at school. We got up to everything and nothing. Walked. Talked. Often we didn't have to say much. We seemed to understand each other intuitively. And there was always music. Anything could be interrupted at any moment for a discussion of which albums Trevor Horn might end up producing next year. We could go from jumping from rock to rock to a conversation about Kraftwerk's early albums with Ralf and Florian. Before Kraftwerk were Kraftwerk. Unless they were actually already Kraftwerk even then?

It soon became apparent that the whole music thing was more than a casual interest to Magnus. He wanted to learn everything, he said. About what was happening now, and what had gone on in the past. Every so often he would ask me to run through the various lineups of different groups and tell him what I thought might happen in the future. Was Alan Wilder likely to stay in Depeche Mode, or would he leave after the next album? And maybe Martin Gore never really felt like a fully fledged member of the group, seeing as he replaced Vince Clarke, who'd been there from the start? What buildings was Jean-Michel Jarre going to perform on next? What was going to happen to the Fun Boy Three now that Terry Hall had started working with the Bananarama girls? Which producers were lined up to work on which groups' next albums? And were they good choices? Was the background you could see on the cover of *Gosh It's . . . Bad Manners* actually a live recording studio? And if so, was that where they recorded "Don't Be Angry"? Did I think we could expect the follow-up to be a live album?

I tried to answer as comprehensively as I could and couldn't help thinking that some of my guesses were pretty well informed.

After a while I started to make special mix tapes that I would mark with different colors. Then I would run through them with Magnus down by the marsh.

We hardly ever spoke about school. But from time to time we would compare our experiences. And I soon figured out that everything was much, much worse at Berg School. In comparison, life at Vira Elementary seemed almost comfortable.

For me it was mostly a question of annoying pranks. For instance, I was given the nickname Ant because I once suggested that ants were one of the strongest animals in the world, which was based on a misunderstanding but caused much hilarity among teacher and pupils, and was later used as a recurrent example of the dangers of mixing up *relative* values with *actual* ones.

But everything was always worse for Magnus.

The same day I got whipped with wet towels in the shower at my school, Magnus got beaten up at Berg. And by that I mean properly beaten up.

In my case it was mostly just high jinks that got out of hand. Dennis or Sören or someone had seen somewhere that if you twisted a wet towel you could make a decent whip, so they tried it out on the Ant while they discussed the best way to get the most force behind their blows.

Obviously they weren't out to get me. But seeing as I was the last person in the shower, I was the only person they could practice on. And they clearly didn't have any idea how much it hurt. I jumped out of the way for as long as I could until they got me so many times that I slipped and fell over. I hit my knee on the tiled floor so hard that I felt something inside crack.

I had to go and see the school nurse, and was sent to the health center to get my knee checked out. The upshot was that I got told off by the PE teacher for running on the slippery tiled floor in the shower.

"We've talked about this enough times," he said as the

rest of the class nodded. "Running in the shower can be lethal. You were lucky it was only your knee this time. Next time it could be this." He slapped me across the head to indicate what he meant.

When I limped over to meet Magnus that afternoon he was in much worse shape. They'd beaten him with sticks in the parking lot behind the school cafeteria. He was a mass of bruises. One of them had brought his stick down right on Magnus's head. He lowered his head and pointed to a large bump with a nasty cut across his scalp. I stared at his battered body.

"You don't think you should go to the hospital?" I said.

"No," he said. "It'll heal."

"Why did they do it?" I asked.

"They're frightened."

"Of what?"

"Me."

"Why are they frightened of you?"

"I don't know. There's just something about me."

"What?"

He shook his head.

"I don't know. Something. What about you?"

"What about me?" I said.

"Yeah?"

"Nothing."

"So why do they hit you?"

"They don't hit me."

"No?"

"Not the way they hit you."

In the end we got bored of the marsh and spent more and more time in my room, sitting on the bed listening to music. Record after record. Looking at album covers and discussing the running order. Analyzing titles. Singing along at the same time, as out of synch as Adam Green and Kimya Dawson in "Steak for Chicken."

It was around then that he showed up with that Roxette album, *Look Sharp!* He thought it had "rhythm." He thought Per and Marie sang well together. That they were kind of "adventurous." I asked if he had learned nothing from me, but he persisted, saying it had its good points and pointing out that I had said it was OK to listen to some chart music. I didn't have the heart to deny him those stupid songs. So we listened to them as well. After a while I got used to it, and even started to appreciate some production aspects, at least on the first album, *Pearls of Passion.*

But I made no mention of this to Dansson.

16

"What about him?" Dansson said as he piled records up beside him.

The Record King was still in the little room behind the counter.

"Oh, I don't know," I said. "He's disappeared."

Dansson looked up at me.

"Roxette? Disappeared?"

"Yes."

"Disappeared, how?"

"I can't get hold of him."

"Really?" Dansson said as he started to look through the jazz section. "Maybe he's killed himself?"

I pushed some records back and leaned against the display.

"Why do you say that?"

"People do it all the time. It's more common than you'd think."

I ran my finger over the records and glanced at Dansson, who was still looking through the jazz.

"So why would he take me to the circus, then?"

"The circus?"

"Yeah . . ."

He looked at me.

"You went to the circus together?" he said, frowning.

"Well, he asked me to go. Then he got involved in one of the acts."

"What sort of act?"

"The magic act, obviously."

"He took part in a magic trick?"

"Yes."

"Did he get sawn in half?"

"No."

"What sort of trick was it, then?"

"Just a normal magic trick."

"With knives?"

"No, mirrors."

Dansson nodded seriously. He repeated what I'd said.

"Mirrors?"

"Yes. Then he didn't come back. And now I can't get hold of him."

Dansson nodded silently to himself. Then he came around to my side of the racks.

"Did he volunteer?" he said.

"How do you mean?"

He looked at me sternly.

"Did he volunteer to take part in the magic act?"

I nodded.

"You know what that means, don't you?" he said.

"No," I said.

"He wanted to make a statement."

The Record King came out behind the counter and put a record by the National up above the till. I did my best to look like I was interested in the stock and tried to spot something I might want to buy, but I couldn't find anything.

As we stepped out onto the street Dansson turned to me and said, "I knew someone who disappeared."

"Oh?" I said.

"And I mean properly disappeared," Dansson went on, fastening his green camouflage army-surplus jacket. "He became invisible."

"What do you mean by invisible?"

"He stopped being visible."

I could feel a laugh bubbling up inside me.

Dansson gave me an affronted look.

"What, don't you believe me?"

"Well . . . like the invisible man or something?"

"I swear. He could disappear. Just like that. When we were at a concert, for instance. One moment you could see him. Next moment he was gone."

"OK . . . ?"

"I've got proof, if you still don't believe me."

"What proof?" I said.

"Photographic proof."

Dansson dug about in the inside pocket of his army

jacket—he seemed to have a lot of things tucked away in there—and eventually pulled out a battered photograph of several people.

"Take a look at this," he said, pointing at the picture. "This was at Hultsfred. When I was there with Nasim, Jovan, Lena, and Tom. Here we all are in front of the main stage."

"So?" I said.

"You can see for yourself. Tom isn't there."

I looked at the picture, and sure enough Tom wasn't there.

I suddenly remembered the note Jallo had given me, and felt for it in my pocket. Yep, there it was, the receipt with Bondegatan 3A on the back. Perhaps it was worth a try?

17

There was no Bondegatan 3A. There was a Bondegatan 3,
an unassuming doorway with a coded lock, but I could see
no sign of a 3A.

Next door was a dry cleaner that might well have the
same address. I went in.

The shop's owner was a man in his fifties, with his hair
pulled into a little ponytail with a beige hairband. I caught
sight of him toward the back in another room. He waved at
me to indicate that he'd seen me but waited awhile before
coming out. There was a bench next to the counter with a
pile of papers and a portable CD player on it. Next to that
was a unsteady stack of CDs that looked like they'd topple
over if you so much as touched the bench. I put my head to
one side and counted seven Absolute Music albums.

In spite of the limited material he had to work with, the
shop's owner still managed to give the impression that he
had lots of hair, and when he turned toward me I saw how
pale he was. It looked almost like he never left his shop.
Perhaps he didn't?

He was wearing one of those pale blue shirts that never

look creased no matter how much they've been worn. The sort of shirt that looks like it came from a discount store, or has been worn and washed so much it has ended up looking like a cheap shirt. Or one that might have been part of some sort of council uniform. White, or very pale blue. The sort of shirt you know is sweaty under the arms even if you can't tell by looking at it. Even if they're covered by a thick jacket, you just know they're wet with sweat.

That sort of shirt only exists for people with sweaty armpits.

The shirt in the back room, with its armpits and associated body, and the head with the long thin hair, slowly began to move, until eventually the whole package was standing in front of me, breathing heavily.

"Yes," he said.

"Is this Bondegatan 3A?" I asked.

The man in the shirt nodded.

"I'm looking for someone called Magnus," I said.

"Magnus?" the shirt said.

"I was told he was here."

He looked at me and scratched his chin.

"Do you want something cleaned?"

"No."

"Oh. There's no Magnus here."

"Magnus Gabrielsson?"

"No."

A short, thickset woman was pulling thin plastic bags over freshly laundered white shirts that had a papery look to them. She was wearing an outfit somewhere between a dress and a cleaner's tunic. I could see her bra through the fabric as she hung the garments up and attached labels to them. She hadn't deigned to look in my direction at all.

These people looked utterly unruffled, but that didn't necessarily mean that they didn't know what I was talking about. Perhaps you had to give some sort of code word, but Jallo hadn't mentioned anything about that. I sighed at his habit of always giving incomplete information and just assuming that things would work themselves out. It was so typical of him, that whole *mañana* attitude. There was no such thing as a problem. Only opportunities. How many times had he tried to recruit me to the telesales business that formed the core of his activities? It covered everything from selling socks and mobile contracts to acting as a kind of emergency psychological helpline.

"You can choose," he kept saying. "Whatever you fancy doing."

With the premium-rate numbers the main point was to keep people talking for as long as possible. According to Jallo that didn't require any special qualifications or experience. All you had to do was keep talking, but that wasn't exactly my strong point.

"Doesn't matter," Jallo said. "If you like you can do the tarot cards. You'd be good at that."

"I don't know anything about tarot."

"You'll soon pick it up. You just have to sit there with the cards and say stuff. The more cryptic the better. That could be your thing . . . quiet and mysterious."

"But it wouldn't be real."

"What the hell is real? Trust me, you'd soon pick it up. They just want someone to talk to."

I looked around the dry cleaner. There was a picture on one wall, the same sort of messy, incomprehensible thing that Jallo had in his office. I found that sort of picture unsettling. I didn't want to spend too long looking at them. They always felt a bit like an optical trap. Colorful patterns that could turn into anything at all when you least expected it. Perhaps the whole dry-cleaning business was just a front? A cover for an entirely different sort of business.

I leaned forward in what I thought was a pointed, conspiratorial way. Like I was trying to let on that I knew what was going on. That I knew about everything, but that they didn't have to worry about me saying anything. I raised one eyebrow.

"Look," I said slowly. "Jallo said it would be OK."

"Jallo?"

I winked and nodded. The man in the shirt stared wearily at me.

"That's nice," he said, equally slowly. "But if you don't

want to have anything dry-cleaned, I'm afraid I can't help you."

He turned around and started to sort through some plastic-wrapped suits.

"Isn't this Bondegatan 3A?" I asked.

"It's number 3. There's no A here."

18

That evening I took a walk past Magnus's flat, but it still looked empty. Abandoned. I stood outside the 7-Eleven for a while looking up at the dark windows. I realized that the window where I'd seen a light go on a few days before might not belong to Magnus. After a while I went into the shop and bought some chewing gum. I sat down in the same place as before and noticed the cashier watching me surreptitiously. Veronica Maggio was playing from the speakers, that song with the line "this situation is so sick." I thought about the girls on the bakery counter, who had asked if I wanted to go to a party this evening. They always asked me when they were going to do something because they knew I had the good sense to decline any offer of socializing with girls who were ten or fifteen years younger than me.

In the street was the same advertisement that was outside my building. The guy in white underpants. Presumably an ad for an underwear company, though it could have been for aftershave or deodorant. Unfortunately for the advertiser, there was a tear in the poster just where the company's name was, so it was impossible to know what brand they wanted you to buy.

I looked up at Magnus's flat again and wondered if he was the sort of person who might commit suicide. Why would he do that? And it would seem odd if he'd done it now. Unnecessary, somehow. At school maybe, but now?

I remembered the badge Magnus used to wear on his breast pocket, LIVE HARD AND DIE YOUNG. That was so wrong. Having a badge like that was ridiculous. Because everyone knew that if there was one thing Magnus didn't do, it was live hard. He didn't drink, didn't smoke, and had hardly ever ridden so much as a moped. He ran around the marsh with me, or sat on my bed listening to records. LIVE HARD AND DIE YOUNG. But it was only a badge. I tried to persuade him to take it off, but he kept wearing it.

A couple came into the shop and bought a bottle of Coke, which they shared between kisses. I sat for a while, feeling tired, and thought of the way Magnus could stand and stare at couples like that without the least embarrassment. He thought it was cute. Sure, when you're a teenager, but you soon learn better. You realize what a nuisance it is once the first flush of infatuation is over, when everything goes back to normal. At best, it might be exciting to begin with, but then the nagging starts, and you have to change your habits, and before you know it the jealousy and arguments start. And even if you think she's attractive and fun, it always ends up leading to loads of problems, no matter how you try to deal with it. Arguments about what to eat and who to see and why you don't want to merge your record collections. If she's got one. And if she hasn't there's always a load of talk about why you have a collection and why can't you just download whatever you feel like listening to? Before you know it you're standing there with tablecloths and curtains and wondering if it's really what you want. You start to argue, get upset, and whatever happiness you once felt turns into pain that's many times worse.

Magnus kept falling in love with girls in a very unhealthy way. He would associate them with a particular type of music, confusing the lyrics of love songs with real life. He saw the lyrics as a way of expressing his love, but hardly ever dared to approach anyone. Then he would see them with other guys and be mortified. Many was the time I had to sit with Magnus trying to comfort him and running through my own thoughts on the subject, usually getting caught up in the horrifying example of my own parents. A long-term relationship that was always on the brink of disharmony, like a drawn-out Allan Pettersson symphony. I kept telling him he needed to learn how things worked. How you make yourself tougher. Untouchable. Otherwise you risk being destroyed. I don't think he ever really learned that.

It soon occurred to me that I ought to go back to the circus and talk to someone there. Maybe they knew where he'd gone. I remembered the old rule from school outings in the forest: that if you got lost or didn't know where everyone else was, you should make your way back to where you last saw them and wait there, hugging a tree or something.

Then I realized I wasn't sure where the circus was. I'd gone there with Magnus, and we spent the whole way talking, so I wasn't paying attention. But presumably it was out on the field a few stations away, where circuses usually pitched their tents.

Live hard and die young. Well, that depends on how you look at things. I slid off my chair and went out into the cool spring air, put my headphones on, and switched on my portable CD player, then set off toward the station. When I went inside I saw that they were working on the escalators down to the platform. A man in a hi-vis jacket gestured to me to take my headphones off.

"What line?" he asked.

I looked down at the CD player.

"Two," I said.

"OK, that way," he said, pointing to a temporary flight of steps.

I walked down it, got on a train, and went the three stations to the circus. I emerged from the end of the station closest to the field, barely even noticing that I had the road to myself. I didn't look up until I reached the grass, when I saw that it was gone. The field was completely empty, the grass standing tall, swaying in the breeze. There was no trace of any tents or caravans.

It was as if the circus had never been there.

19

That night the phone rang again.

"Magnus?" I said, but there was no response. Just the nervous breathing. Was it someone from the circus?

"Magnus, is that you?" I asked again.

No response.

I went and sat down in front of the television without switching it on. I sat there for a long time looking at my own shadow on the screen, feeling the presence of the silent person on the telephone line. After several minutes, during which neither of us said anything, I went over to the stereo and put on "Lilac Wine" by Jeff Buckley and held the receiver up to the speaker.

When the track ended I hung up and walked into the bedroom, lay down on top of the bed, and leafed through the latest issue of *Uncut*. Nothing in it really caught my attention. I was having trouble concentrating. How could the circus be gone all of a sudden? Was it possible to move an entire cavalcade of people and vehicles in such a way that they didn't leave any trace of having been there? Surely the grass at least ought to have been flattened? Shouldn't there be a few scraps of circus detritus about the place, a bit of tinsel or a plastic cup and a few napkins from the kiosk? Why didn't the person who kept calling me say anything, and what had Magnus meant when he waved like that in the mirror?

I must have dozed off, because the next time I opened my eyes it was dark inside the flat. I sat up, stared at the pitch-black room, and wasn't altogether sure if I was asleep or awake. But I thought it was odd for the phone to be ringing in a dream. It rang and rang and rang—an old-fashioned ringtone. I answered. It was Magnus.

"Hello?" I said.

"Hello, this is Magnus Gabrielsson. But a long time ago."

"Oh?" I said.

"I was wondering if you've got Kurt Cobain's number. From when he was a child?"

20

The next day was a day in which nothing happened. Noth-ing out of the ordinary, anyway. Only the sort of thing you might expect to happen on a Wednesday.

I woke up, went to work, worked, had lunch.

It was the sort of day when I saw stir-fried noodles and thought they looked tempting, and then saw stir-fried noo-dles and thought they looked disgusting, and in between those reactions nothing much happened apart from me eat-ing rather a lot of stir-fried noodles.

I tried putting Sheena Easton between Prince and Wendy and Lisa because it ought to work—theoretically, anyway—but it didn't feel right at all.

In the end I decided to do what Jallo had suggested and try writing a letter. I got a pen and some paper and sat down to write.

"Dear Magnus!" I began, then wondered if that sounded too pompous, before concluding that it didn't matter. I couldn't let myself get bogged down in that sort of detail. The important thing was to get in touch with him. Not the tone of the letter itself. Besides, I thought it sounded rather nice. "Dear Magnus!" Kind of ceremonial. It felt good to write it. I concluded with "Best wishes."

When I was finished I dug out an envelope, wrote his address on it, added a stamp, and went and mailed it.

I spent the rest of the afternoon with Dictaphone and their album *Poems from a Rooftop*.

It was the sort of day that passed like any other, and I reasoned that Magnus Gabrielsson couldn't possibly have committed suicide. I got confirmation of that the following day.

21

I spent all of Thursday behind the bakery counter hum-ming "Dinner at Eight" by Rufus Wainwright as I served the old women who wanted pastries and cakes in the shape of graduation caps. I was glad it wasn't "Love and Marriage" and wondered if perhaps "Dinner at Eight" might have the opposite effect.

When I got to Record King after work I spent a while searching for the Rufus Wainwright album I'd seen the other day but couldn't find it anywhere. Could it really have been sold? Had Record King had a customer?

I walked home and sang out loud to myself in a Rufus Wainwright style as I changed into a shirt that I soon discovered smelled of sweat, so I had to change back again.

I tried moving the whole Motown section down three shelves but quickly realized that that messed up the other end, where part of old-style hip-hop ended up next to Americana, so I had to move the whole lot back again.

Then I wolfed down some sweet corn straight from the tin I'd opened the night before last. It tasted a bit metallic but not too bad. I shook my head and chuckled at the thought of She & Him next to Young MC. I didn't really feel like going out but felt I ought to for Dansson's sake.

A bit further along the same street as Record King lay what, back in the glory days of vinyl, used to be the Record King Bar but was now an Irish theme pub. It wasn't called the Record King Bar anymore, but it still had pretty much the same clientele and fairly decent music, and it was where the Record King was apparently going to DJ.

I ordered a beer and sat down at the bar beside an empty stool to indicate that I was waiting for someone. I hoped Dansson would show up soon.

I was left sitting there on my own for a long time, listening to the music. I thought about asking the Record King to play "Dinner at Eight" if he had it, but decided against it. I'd never asked a DJ to play anything, and I wasn't about to start now. I got another beer and thought about an article about vinyl collectors I'd read at a newsstand. I'd just started to get annoyed at the memory of the phrase "airy quality to the sound" when someone interrupted my musings.

In the middle of Jeff Beck's "You Had It Coming," Janne Markstedt was suddenly standing in front of me waving his hands. I lit up the way you do when you meet someone you haven't seen for several years and are expected to want to know all about them.

"Janne?!" I said.

"That's me." He grinned. "It's been a while!"

There was something so familiar about him, something that had always been there and probably always would be. The way he moved his head and spoke, his whole body language. The hard-rock attitude. But I could see how old he'd got. A proper grown-up with gray hair and a receding hairline. When did that happen? I'd always assumed we were the same age. It felt like it, especially as we'd been in the same class and everything.

I didn't know what to say, so I asked loudly, "You doing OK?"

"Good," he said. I noticed that he was swaying slightly to the sound of the guitar from the speakers.

"Good to see you again," he said after a while. "Do you still see anyone else from school?"

"No, not really," I said. "You know how it is."

I thought about how I did my best to avoid anything connected to the past and only saw Jallo and Magnus from those days. I thought about what Janne had meant to me at school. Essentially nothing, aside from being part of the crowd of hard-rock fans who always trailed after Dennis and his gang. The ones who kept quiet and watched.

Janne nodded as if he understood. Even if he couldn't possibly have heard what I'd said. Then he frowned and pulled a face.

"Shit, I heard about that guy, your friend Magnus!" he yelled.

"What about him?" I yelled back.

"That guy, Magnus. He was a friend of yours, wasn't he?"

"What d'you mean?"

"Awful business."

"What?"

"Him committing suicide," he said.

I choked on my beer and started to cough. Janne leaned forward to slap me on the back, but I held up my hand to stop him.

"What?" I yelled when I'd stopped coughing.

"Not that I really knew him or anything, but it's terrible, isn't it? Hadn't you heard?" Janne yelled back.

I stared at him.

"How?" I said. He leaned forward.

"At the circus."

I grabbed hold of the table, took a swig of beer, and shook my head.

Janne went on shouting in my ear.

"Cut himself on some glass."

"Glass?"

"Yeah. From a mirror."

"Where?"

"At the circus. Apparently he walked out into the middle of a magic trick and did it there and then. Can you imagine? The magician was distraught."

"How do you know all this?"

"Well . . . from what I heard, it was supposed to be some sort of political statement."

I couldn't stay after that. I was too upset to sit in the pub, so after another few minutes of Janne shouting about former classmates right next to my ear I said I had to go to the toilet. I took my jacket and walked out. Dansson still hadn't turned up. Why didn't I have any normal friends?

I wandered along the pavement in the darkness, in and out of patches of light of varying brightness as they reflected off the puddles, and felt my skin tighten. Janne was clearly a bit of a gossip, and it wasn't hard to figure out who he'd got his information from, but Magnus Gabrielsson *was* missing. That was a fact. So where was he, if he hadn't killed himself?

I could feel I was a bit drunk and wondered if I was going to start crying. Poor Magnus, I thought. Where have you got to? My heart was pounding. I realized I was almost running. I slowed down and took a couple of deep breaths. Tried to think about my record collection, but not even that could improve my mood. Was this how it had started for Magnus as well? I wondered.

* * *

I didn't notice how odd Magnus was until Year 7 or 8. I knew he was a bit unusual, but up until then we had our own world, where nothing ever needed to be compared to anything outside it. Where everything seemed normal, no matter how peculiar it was. But somewhere around the start of secondary school it finally dawned on me that Magnus was different. More different than even I was.

To start with, he was genuinely frightened of other people. Almost reclusive. I started to wonder if he ever went to school at all. His old rucksack usually hung slack, as if it was empty. I never saw any schoolbooks, and he was never in a rush to get home and do his homework. If I ever suggested we meet up with anyone else he would glance at his digital watch and say he had to be somewhere else. If we ever had anyone else with us he never said much and would always come up with some excuse and hurry away.

His personal hygiene wasn't great, and sometimes he smelled. The carefree, undemanding, fun existence we shared slowly changed into a sort of mutual boredom. He never wanted to try anything new, just carry on doing the same childish things we'd always done, even though we were getting older and older. In the end it felt embarrassing. We started to annoy each other. Started arguing about stupid things. What groups it was OK to like, that sort of thing. His firm views about what was synth music and what wasn't began to feel more and more stifling.

"But we listen to lots of different things," he said in an accusing tone.

"We listen to things that are good," I said.

"That means you can listen to all sorts of things," he said.

"Not any old thing, only things that are good," I said.

"So how do you know what's good, then?"

It usually ended with me getting my way, but even that never felt great. Magnus didn't seem to have any will of his own. It was like he was happy doing nothing and just letting me decide. In the end we would just sit at either end of the bed in my room listening to records, neither of us saying anything. There wasn't much to say. It was nice and non-threatening, but got kind of boring after a while. Even if Magnus didn't seem to think so.

"Can we listen to the whole of *Tubular Bells* again?" he said.

"I suppose so," I said.

So we did.

It felt a bit like being married. Or what people say being married is like. That you always have to stay at home, sit at the kitchen table talking about the same old things you've already talked about a thousand times before. Never going out with friends, and if you did feeling guilty for spending time with other people. And I thought I was too young to be married. To someone like Magnus, anyway. It annoyed me that he always had to be so antisocial. So timid.

As time went by I started to wish he was a bit tougher. Or at least a bit more extroverted. It was hard to meet girls, for instance. If I had Magnus with me, anyway. He had very firm views on the women he wanted to meet and how this should happen, and who should say what and in what order. But if an opportunity ever arose he always walked away. And most of the time he wanted me to go with him.

He didn't have any choice, of course. He didn't know any better. He didn't have anyone else but me. Even so, I ended up seeing less and less of him. Sometimes I took my headphones off and talked to someone at school instead. Discussing homework, or telling them what was on the lunch menu that day. Stuff like that. There was another life outside the claustrophobic little world Magnus and I had constructed. Even if it wasn't always easy. In my case it tended to involve a lot of recurring practical jokes. Nothing too terrible. It was more like a form of shorthand. I was the one everyone made fun of. And with time I learned to deal with that a bit better. I started to play along, basically.

There were times when I felt accepted, if not exactly popular. Sometimes it was even quite fun. Not that I ever made jokes or anything like that, but I could get others to laugh. I came up with silly stuff like letting them pull my suspenders until they snapped back and hit me. Or running into a wall. I did that a lot, and it would get a laugh from someone. I would simply run as fast as I could straight into a wall.

Once when we were standing by our lockers I punched my clenched fist into the door of my locker as hard as I could. People began to stare. Dennis and Sören cheered each time the door buckled, and I was so buoyed up by the response that I kept doing it until the blood from my knuckles began to smear across the door.

Magnus never understood any of that. He couldn't understand that you sometimes had to give away a little bit of yourself. He thought that was selling out. Whenever I told him about something like that he would give me a derisive glare. As if he had some sort of right to judge me. As if he had the right to look down on me just because I was adapting and making a bit of an effort. Unlike certain other people. Even though he never said anything, I could hear what he was thinking. I didn't share his attitude. Sometimes I ended up shouting at him because of it. And then I'd feel guilty. As if I'd done something wrong. As if I'd let someone down.

Either way, it did seem to work.

One morning I got a chance to talk to Dennis. We arrived at one of the school entrances at the same time; the doors were supposed to be open but for some reason they were still locked. Dennis banged on the glass. He asked what sort of music I listened to. I mentioned a few names. He probably didn't know any of them. We stood there together for a while. A couple of minutes at least. In the end he asked if he could listen to my headphones.

I quickly checked which tape was in the Walkman and decided that it would probably be OK. I passed him the headphones. Ideally it would have been one of the hardcore compilations, but it was the Blue Mix. Propaganda, Yazoo, Bronski Beat, and Soft Cell. Well, it would just have to do. Dennis nodded. He took hold of the Walkman and put the headphones on his big head. He swayed a little in time to the music. Seemed happy.

"Decent sound," he said, slightly too loudly. "Can I borrow this?"

No, absolutely not. Under no circumstances. No one was allowed to borrow it. My Walkman was my refuge at school. My own space. My sanctuary. I'd rather have lent someone my mother or Magnus or all my savings if I had any. But not my Walkman. My Walkman was an extension of me. That music and those songs formed the whole structure of my existence.

But this was Dennis asking, and obviously that changed everything.

Others were bound to be impressed that Dennis was

borrowing things from me. He looked so happy as he stood there with the headphones on. Almost expectant. It was as if the music—*my* music—had got through to him. Had changed his attitude to synth music. To me. It was impossible to turn him down. Maybe this was the start of . . . well, if not friendship, then at least a form of admittance into the gang.

Because of course I could see a parallel. This was exactly how my friendship with Magnus had started. Now things weren't so great with Magnus, maybe this was the natural next step? Maybe it was going to be me and Dennis from now on? The thought of him walking around with my Walkman and mentioning my name in relation to the tracks he was listening to made me ecstatic. And it would mean we had a reason to meet up again soon.

On the other side of the glass the caretaker was hurrying to unlock the doors with his big bunch of keys. This was my chance, and I had to decide quickly. The doors would soon be open and the encounter would be over.

"OK," I said. "But I need it back after school."

"Sweet," Dennis said and slipped in through the doors before we had arranged where and when I was going to get it back.

I spent the rest of the day on a peculiar high. I felt naked without music in my ears. All sounds seemed unnaturally loud and intrusive. It made it hard to think. I was having to feel my way through a whole new world, but I still felt oddly carefree. Because I had a secret understanding with Dennis now, even if we didn't actually talk at all—of course we didn't; everything was more or less the same as usual, you can't change things that quickly—but it still made me see him in a different light. In a lot of ways Dennis was a far more rounded person than Magnus. Sociable. Talented. A natural leader. Top grades in math and science. All the subjects I was worst at. I was best at the humanities. He and I could be a really good combination.

I felt like I'd been given an invitation. To a tougher world, sure, but one that was also more complicated and interesting. Wild and unpredictable. Maybe I needed to make my way out into this noisy, messy, stormy world in order to take my place in . . . real life?

At the same time the music would start to work from the other direction. The tracks that Dennis was listening to now, they were a potential bridge between us. They would slowly bring us closer together. He couldn't help but be swept along by the percussion intro to "Sorry for Laughing." Or the grinding bass of "p:Machinery," which just kept going until it eventually gave you goosebumps. If he listened to the recurring brass riff at the end of the track he'd never be able to forget it. Or when Dave Gahan sings "It's just a question of time" on the *Black Celebration* album. I could offer to make him some mix tapes of his own, I thought. I could do that for him. I saw myself explaining the greatness of one track after the other. The unlikely combination of the two of us could be positive for him too. Maybe that was what he'd had in mind when he approached me that morning. Even if he might not have been aware of it himself. Maybe it was a subconscious desire on his part to expand his taste in music. After all, he'd taken the first step . . . Was this the start of us becoming civilized adults who socialized properly and learned from each other? Who saw the differences between us as something positive, as opportunities to expand our horizons?

We could share the Walkman, I thought. Have it every other day. Obviously the days without it would be tough, but it would be fun to make mix tapes if I knew he was going to go around listening to them. And he could make tapes too. Was this the moment when synth and hard rock met? The first step to a musical dialogue? After all, I had already started listening to a bit of Rush and Van Halen, in spite of Magnus's protests, and to my ears they sounded like rock. So I'd begun to sound out the terrain, so to speak. I'd have to remember to mention that to Dennis. And of course I'd have to identify some synth tracks that could build a bridge to hard rock. I started to think out a suitable playlist for the first mix tape.

During break I saw him demonstrating the Walkman to some girls in the class and realized that it would be easier to gain access to them now as well.

It was a delicate situation, one that needed to be handled correctly. I had to do my bit to make it easy for him. Not push myself forward too soon. Not try to snatch victory too early. He had his reputation to think about, after all. Obviously he couldn't be seen with someone like me. He stood to lose everything from a change of that sort. In the short term, anyway. The transition needed to happen gradually, almost imperceptibly. That wasn't the sort of thing you can change overnight, so the best thing for the time being was to lie low for a while and let the friendship between us develop so slowly that no one would notice how the two of us came to be in each other's proximity. Swapping mix tapes and discussing different tracks.

I kept my distance all day. As did Dennis. Even if he made it look like he wasn't trying.

At the end of the day I went down to the lockers at the same time as everyone else for a change. I hung back slightly, looking for Dennis. When he showed up with the headphones around his neck and the Walkman on his belt I went toward him. I wasn't planning on hanging around. I just wanted to see if it was time for him to give the Walkman back. It could have happened almost unnoticed. Almost without words. Then obviously I'd have walked away. But before I got that far Sören Ranebo was standing in front of me.

"What do you want?" he said, pushing me back. Not

hard, but enough for me to sway and lose my balance slightly.

"I'm just going to collect something," I said.

"What sort of something?" he said.

"Something that . . . belongs to me," I said.

"No you're not," Sören said and pushed me again.

Not hard, but enough to let me know that my path was blocked.

I could see Dennis up ahead, and waited for him to turn toward us and say that it was all OK. That the rules had changed. As soon as he saw who it was he'd come and sort it all out. Give me back my Walkman, and the whole thing would be something of a triumph. (Eventually even Sören Ranebo would come to terms with the fact that synth and rock were on the point of a rapprochement.) But people kept going up to Dennis and talking to him. He was surrounded by admirers. I saw them fiddling with the Walkman and headphones.

"Get lost!" Sören said.

"But . . . ," I said.

"Something wrong with your hearing? Get lost, I said!" Sören said, pushing me again. Harder this time, making me stumble and fall on my backside. He probably didn't intend it, but I landed on my coccyx and jarred my spine.

I sat there as the others moved on, thinking to myself that it was probably best to hold off a bit longer and try to make contact with Dennis when there weren't so many people around him.

I followed them at a discreet distance. Saw them go in and out of shops. Maybe they did a bit of shoplifting in Åhlén's? The headphones kept getting passed around the gang, but Dennis kept hold of the Walkman, which I thought he seemed to be handling carefully.

In the end there were only three of them left, and when they were sitting on a bench in the shopping center I ventured closer. I saw Dennis look in my direction, and before I realized how stupid it was I'd already raised my arm in a far too enthusiastic greeting. I lowered it at once and walked toward them.

Sören had gone, but one of the boys in the parallel class, I think his name was Johan—his dad had a Commodore 64—stood up as I approached.

"What do you want?" he said.

"Er . . . I thought I'd pick up my Walkman," I said.

"What did you say?" Johan said, raising his eyebrows.

He turned his ear toward me as if he couldn't hear properly.

"I'd just like my Walkman back," I mumbled.

"Who's got it?" he said with a grin.

I glanced at Dennis and the other boy, who were sitting on the bench looking at us. I thought that maybe this was Dennis's style, keeping you on tenterhooks. Sending one of his minions to test you, like a sort of initiation rite. You just had to make sure you passed it. Stayed cool in front of his friends. Even so, I was unable to keep as cool as I would have liked. I tried to smile, but it felt more like a nervous twitch.

"Where's your Walkman?" Johan asked again.

I looked at him, then at the other boy. In the end I pointed to the Walkman in Dennis's hand.

"No. That's Dennis's Walkman," Johan said, shaking his head. "You can't have that. That would be stealing, wouldn't it? You know the difference between 'yours' and 'mine,' don't you?"

"Er," I said. "Look . . . it's mine."

"Dennis's Walkman is yours?" Johan asked with another grin.

I was still waiting for Dennis to give some sort of signal, but he just sat there looking idly in our direction. Every so often he said something to the guy next to him. As if he was commenting on what was going on between me and Johan.

"See for yourself," I said. "That's my tape in it."

"Really?" Johan said. "What tape is it, then?"

I didn't want to say out loud.

"It's got a label on it . . ."

"What tape is it?" he asked again.

" 'Blue Mix'," I said, almost in a whisper. "That's what it says on the label."

He brightened up.

" 'Blue Mix'?"

I nodded. He grinned at me. Then he turned to the others.

"The tape in the Walkman, is it called 'Blue Mix'?"

Dennis opened it up to reveal an original Iron Maiden cassette.

"Sorry," Johan said. "No 'Blue Mix.'"

Dennis closed the lid and Johan shrugged. What had they done with my tape? I wondered. Had they thrown it away?

"But it's mine," I squeaked.

Johan's smile vanished and he looked at me as if he was bored now.

"Are you saying Dennis stole it?"

"No," I said, shaking my head. "I let him borrow it, but now I need it back."

"You need it?! Dear oh dear, these are very serious allegations," Johan said, turning to the two boys on the bench.

He called to Dennis.

"The Ant says you stole it from him."

"Er, no . . . ," I muttered.

I cursed my own impatience. This was the very situation we were supposed to be avoiding, Dennis and I. We were supposed to do this slowly. Let it develop naturally. (Letting synth and hard rock slowly but surely get closer to each other.) That was what I'd been telling myself all day. If only I'd been a bit more patient, this could all have been avoided. Who knows, maybe Dennis had his own idea of how we should proceed? Maybe he'd been thinking of an even slower pace, which I'd now gone and ruined with my impatience. Now he was bound to realize what a mistake it had been to trust someone like me. I'd made a fool of myself, but it occurred to me that I didn't care about him, and I didn't care about any big change. I just wanted to curl up inside my music again, as usual.

"I just want my Walkman back," I whined.

I could hear that I sounded like a little kid.

"But that isn't your Walkman," Johan spelled out very slowly. "You're making it up. It's just your imagination."

He tapped my head with his finger.

"You need to learn to tell the difference between fantasy and reality," he said.

The boy who had been sitting next to Dennis stood up and came over to us.

"Are you accusing Dennis of stealing?" he said.

He stopped right in front of me and stared at me hard. I didn't know what to say.

"Are you? Are you accusing Dennis of stealing?" he said again.

Without blinking he slapped my face hard, making my ear sting. I gasped. Everything was happening so quickly. Now he was talking again.

"Are you standing there accusing Dennis of stealing?" he said in a very calm voice.

My cheek hurt badly. I was having trouble thinking.

"I want—" I started to say, but before I could finish the sentence he'd hit me again. I had to crouch down, and felt tears spring to my eyes.

I could have run off, I could even have walked away calmly. No one would have stopped me. But the Walkman in Dennis's hand belonged to me. And that was more important than anything else just then. So I didn't move.

"Please, I only want—"

He hit me on the same cheek again. I screamed like a baby as he went on speaking in the same calm voice. As if his voice had nothing to do with his hand. As if one person was talking to me and another one hitting me.

"I just want to know," the soft voice went on. "Are you accusing Dennis of stealing? Is that what you're doing?"

Even though my cheek was burning, I couldn't just walk away and abandon my Walkman. I couldn't see clearly. I realized I was crying. I was about to say something but thought better of it.

In utter panic I tried to run forward and snatch the Walkman, but there was obviously no point. Johan and the other boy dragged me away without any difficulty at all. One held me while the other punched me in the stomach, then told me I had to apologize.

23

It had been a long time since I last thought about those events. They weren't the sort of thing I chose to dwell on from day to day. But on the way home from the Record King Bar I was unable to keep all the memories and images from coming back to me. Instead of going straight up to my flat I went out into the back courtyard and sat down on one of the benches in the play area. I just sat there. As if I were going to smoke a cigarette. It was still light even though it was the middle of the night. I could hear the distant rumble of the highway mixed with the sounds of students celebrating their graduation at parties in various flats nearby. It was a lovely early summer's night, perfect for balcony drinking and skinny-dipping in murky water. I slid partway off the seat and rested my neck on the back of the bench. I half-lay like that, looking up at the light sky, where I could just start to make out a few stars.

For the first time I felt that I not only had a life ahead of me, but one behind me as well. A life I could never get back. Summer nights swimming with girls and graduation caps and dreams of the future. Youth unemployment, happiness at getting a first job, all the anxiety and expectation. It wasn't only my childhood that had passed, but the start of my adult life.

I tried to remember the names of as many constellations as I could. What were they called again? Ursa Major and Minor. The Plow. No, that was something else. Besides, it was the wrong time of year to be able to see those.

I was struck by the immense distances between the stars out in space. They only look like they belong together when you see them from a distance. They could hardly be aware that they form part of a constellation, I thought. If stars were conscious, that is. It takes one hell of a distance to be able to see the connection. From the perspective of the stars, Magnus Gabrielsson and I must look like one single indistinguishable little dot, for instance. And if you didn't know better, you could probably say I had a certain type of connection with the person who kept calling me.

24

Mum yelled at me for losing my Walkman. She said I caused them more than enough expense as it was. I couldn't bring myself to explain that I'd lent it to someone. Besides, she made it very clear that there was no question of me getting another one. We didn't have that sort of money, she said. Then she added that it might not be a bad idea for me to get used to not having headphones glued to my head the whole time.

"You need to get out into the real world a bit more," she said.

"We can get it back if there's two of us," I said to Magnus the next day.

We were sitting by the marsh with empty silence ringing in our ears. Throwing stones in the air and listening to them plop wearily into the water. Magnus was leaning against a tree trunk with his knees pulled up to his chin, his nose resting on one knee. The days without my Walkman were completely different. It was like entering an unknown world with different rules. Nothing made sense anymore. Even Magnus was different. Smaller, paler. Scared and nervous. I hadn't seen as much of him recently. He missed the music, obviously.

"We can overpower him," I said. "If we work together."

"What about the others?" Magnus said.

"We'll have to wait until he's alone."

"When?"

"He has to be on his own at some point," I said.

"It won't work," Magnus said.

"Why not?"

He shook his head.

"It just won't. There's no point."

"Of course there is. If there are two of us and one of him. We overpower him and take it back."

Magnus buried his chin between his knees.

"But what if it *isn't* yours?" he said. "I mean, it wasn't your tape in it . . ."

"Of course it's mine," I said. "I let him borrow it."

He sighed.

"Can't you just buy a new one?"

"With what?"

"Steal one."

Magnus sometimes shoplifted. I never did. No one ever noticed him. It was as if he were invisible. Magnus was far too unassuming for anyone to suspect him of committing a crime. He could calmly pay for his one-krona sweets with-

out anyone suspecting that his pockets were full of chocolate bars, lollipops, and batteries. Sometimes even music
magazines.

"No," I said. "Of course we could take him. If we work
together."

I kicked at an old metal locker that was floating at the
edge of the marsh. Magnus frowned. He sighed and let out
a groan.

"If we do it together," I said, "he won't stand a chance!"

Eventually he agreed for us to have a go the following day.
We planned the whole thing in minute detail. Worked out
what order everything should happen in. Jump him, ideally
without him realizing we were coming. I'd hold him while
Magnus grabbed the Walkman. Once he had it he'd give me
a signal and we'd run off. We practiced a few different kicks
and punches behind the old paint warehouse. Told each
other it was vital to withstand any counterpunches he might
manage to throw if he tried to defend himself. Withstand
the pain and not buckle under the first blow.

"It's going to hurt," I said, but somehow that didn't feel
so bad anymore.

It would just have to hurt. After all, everything hurt.

"Blue Mix!" Johan yelled when he caught sight of me the
next day.

I started and looked at him. I wondered if he could tell I was planning something.

"Hello! Blue Mix! Have you found your Walkman yet?"

I didn't answer.

Dennis was still going around with the Walkman on his belt. It did actually look newer than mine. Brighter yellow, somehow. So what? Maybe he'd polished it. I tried to keep out of their way for the rest of the day.

When school was over I met Magnus at the usual place outside the post office. He was nervous and paranoid. Kept looking at his watch and talking nonstop. I kept having to tell him to be quiet.

We found Dennis and his gang and started to follow them. There was a big group of them for a long time, all walking in that assured, confident way they had. It was hard to maintain the right distance—either we hung back too far and risked losing them, or else we risked being seen.

"Look," Magnus whispered. "Why don't we just go home instead?"

"No chance," I said.

Eventually some of them drifted away, but Dennis and Johan seemed to live in the same area, because they continued walking together. They were heading down a long road of detached houses, each one bigger than the last, looming over the road. They were talking and laughing, and pretend-fighting in a pretty rough way. We crept after them.

At regular intervals Magnus prodded me and said we ought to give up.

"It's never going to work," he said, twisting his watch. "Let's just leave it."

There was something so utterly helpless about him. So defenseless. Evasive. Almost as if he wanted us to fail. That annoyed me and made me even more irrationally determined to go through with the attempt.

"Not a chance!" I said as sternly as I could.

"It's never going to work," he went on muttering, like a mantra.

"Of course it will," I said.

The sun was starting to go down over the big detached houses and their neat gardens and Volvo station wagons parked out in the street next to big mailboxes or in the drives and big garages in gardens adorned with hammocks and flagpoles. Some even had tarpaulin-covered swimming pools.

Eventually the two boys ahead of us high-fived each other and Dennis play-punched Johan on the shoulder. Then he carried on along the road alone. It was fairly late by now and Magnus and I were able to creep pretty close to him under cover of the growing darkness.

"Now!" I whispered. "Now, fuck it!"

Magnus stopped and shook his head.

"No," he said.

I stared at him.

"Come on! Let's do it!" I hissed.

Dennis was already walking off. Maybe he lived nearby? If we hesitated now he'd be gone. The opportunity would be wasted and everything would be lost.

"Come on!" I said, a bit louder.

But Magnus just stood there shaking his head. Terrified. Paralyzed. He was actually shaking. He wasn't even looking at his watch, just shaking his head and clenching his hands in front of his groin. He was pressing his legs together. I realized that he'd wet himself. A dark patch spread across his jeans. I realized I was never going to persuade him to go along with this. It wasn't going to happen.

There was no way I could deal with Dennis on my own. He'd make mincemeat of me. But I was too full of adrenaline. And my Walkman was so close. I watched Dennis as he moved slowly but surely farther and farther away, then made a snap decision and ran after him on my own.

I caught up with him just as he was turning to walk through a tall hedge surrounding a large house.

"Dennis!" I shouted, and when I reached the drive I saw that he'd stopped in front of the carport.

He turned. Stared at me, and I thought I could detect a hint of anxiety, or at least surprise, before he realized who it was.

"What the fuck are you doing here?" he said.

We stood there for a few seconds while I wondered if I should launch myself at him or wait and try to gain some sort of advantage. He was only a centimeter or two taller than me, but the odds were still heavily stacked in his favor.

"Did you want something, or what?" Dennis said after a while.

The Walkman was strapped to his belt, shimmering yellow. Only a meter or so away from me. I could have reached out and grabbed it. It would all have been so simple if that bloody traitor Magnus had been there. He wouldn't even have had to do anything, I thought. Just be there. If only he'd been there, I thought.

"I just want my Walkman back," I said in the end.

Dennis merely grinned. A broad smile that showed both rows of teeth. Then he turned, walked up the steps, and went inside the house without another word. I was left standing on the drive. I stood there for a long time after he'd gone.

I didn't see Magnus again that evening. If he'd shown his face I would probably have punched him. Hard. I walked back the same way and thought I heard rustling in the bushes. I called out a few times so that he'd hear me if he was nearby. "You're so fucking useless!" I yelled. "Completely fucking useless!"

I ignored Magnus after that. I walked past him outside the post office, pretending he didn't exist. At first he left me alone, but after a few days he ran up alongside me on the path home from school, whining for forgiveness and coming up with all sorts of pathetic excuses. His foot had started to hurt, he said. It had been too dark. He had been unsure of the plan, thought we were going to wait a bit longer. It hadn't turned out so badly, had it? And so on. Every so often he tried to grab me to make me stop. He was crying and sniveling, but I pulled loose and walked home, without so much as looking at him.

Dennis carried on wearing the Walkman on his belt. There were moments when I couldn't help thinking that I'd made a mistake, that I'd imagined the whole thing. That I'd never lent it to him. Or that I'd lent it to him and then got it back, only to lose it myself and blame it all on Dennis. In which case it was hardly surprising that he and his friends were pissed off with me. I started to get used to the idea, until it almost seemed more likely than the alternative. I could hear Motörhead and Slayer playing on it. Mine had never played groups like that. Eventually I managed to persuade my mum to get me another one—a different make, and a more basic model, but still: it worked. Whenever Magnus appeared I turned the volume up and pretended not to see him. As time passed it got easier and easier to ignore him. In the end it was almost as if he'd disappeared.

25

After sitting on the bench for a fairly long time I started to feel cold and went up to my flat. I realized I was waiting for the silent caller to phone me again. I sat there staring into the darkness, clutching the phone like a stuffed toy or a rosary. It was a long time ago now. It was all such a long time ago. In a way it had been surprisingly easy just to ignore Magnus back then. I simply made my mind up and tuned out the frequency on which his voice was audible. I concentrated on my music instead. If I decided he didn't exist, then he didn't. I soon realized what power I had over him. Without me he was nothing. Sometimes it was almost comforting to know that he was suffering on his own. Because obviously I could take him back at any moment. If I wanted to. Back then I was the one who decided what the rules were.

Now it was him. And he was gone.

I'd just made up my mind to call Magnus again, even though it was after three o'clock in the morning. I caught sight of myself in the black screen of the television. It almost felt like it was him in the television, about to call me. It looked like he was waiting for something. He'll call any moment now, I thought.

Sure enough, the phone rang a short while later. I was raising my hand to answer when I saw that the man in the television already had the receiver pressed to his ear. I did the same.

I was about to ask if he was still alive when I heard a click at the other end, then some crackling, and then "Dinner at Eight" by Rufus Wainwright played on a poor-quality sound system.

26

I listened. To the whole track. I sat there perfectly still and enjoyed it. Like when you're given a present you've always wanted or a genuine compliment or a big hug. Eventually the song came to an end. There was a click, then there was no one there. I hung up, almost certain that the person at the other end was a friend.

But was it Magnus Gabrielsson? And how could he play Rufus Wainwright if he was dead? And if he wasn't dead, which seemed more likely, why would he be playing Rufus Wainwright? Did he even know who he was? Magnus had clung to a fairly fundamentalist line when it came to what music he listened to. There was no place for Rufus Wainwright there. Whoever was playing music at the other end of the line wasn't the Magnus I knew. It was a different one. Unless it was someone else altogether? In which case, who?

I went over to my computer and did a search for Magnus Gabrielsson.

* * *

I tried typing in Magnus's phone number, and found both his name and address. So he does exist, I thought rather stupidly. But the person on the phone didn't feel like Magnus. Magnus would never sit in silence and then play "Dinner at Eight." Anyway, how could anyone else know about "Dinner at Eight"? I hadn't mentioned to anyone that I'd been thinking about it. Coincidence? Maybe, but it was more likely that someone had picked up on me humming it. The girls at work? A customer? Dansson? Anyway, how loud was my humming? Did I really walk about singing to myself?

After a while the phone rang again. I answered on the first ring. Neither of us said anything. I went over to the stereo, switched it on, then held the receiver up as I played "Who Are You?" by Scarlett Johansson.

27

The next morning I called Dansson from the phone at work. I waited until I was alone in the employee changing room, then sat on the bench leaning back against the lockers. I had a headache and could feel the sweat on my back.

"Have you heard anything about Magnus Gabrielsson?" I said as soon as he answered.

"Roxette?" he said blearily.

"What have you heard?" I said.

I heard Dansson breathe heavily into the phone.

"That he committed suicide, you mean?"

"Who did you hear that from?"

"You. Among others."

"Who else?"

"Well . . . you, anyway."

My head was throbbing, and I thought I'd better try to find a painkiller.

"I didn't say that," I said.

"No? What did you say, then?"

"I said he'd disappeared."

"Oh?"

"That's one hell of a difference."

I closed my eyes and tried to calm down.

"Has anyone else said anything about him?" I asked after a short pause.

"Don't think so," Dansson said.

"Seriously, has anyone said anything?"

"No," Dansson said. "What the hell—can I go back to sleep now?"

28

That evening the phone rang again. At first the line was silent. Just that same breathing. It felt simultaneously creepy and exciting, kind of forbidden. As if Magnus and I, if it was him, had found an entirely new way to communicate.

This time I was ready. I'd made it a bit of an occasion. I'd bought a bar of chocolate and broken it into squares, but left it in the wrapper so I could have some whenever I felt like it. I popped a piece in my mouth as I went over to the record shelves, wondering what to play.

I pulled out both Fink's *Sort of Revolution* and Matthew E. White's "One of These Days," but before I had time to choose a track I heard noises at the other end of the line, then "This Is Killing Me" by Skid Row started to play.

I concentrated on listening. What did he mean by "This Is Killing Me"? What was killing him? Was he in some sort of dangerous situation after all? Was that why he couldn't talk? Maybe he could only play music and was using it to send coded messages to me? Should I inform the authorities? Or was it his kidnapper playing the music?

Skid Row? I thought for a long time before finally put-

ting on "Who Am I Talking To" from Andy Pratt's epony-
mous album.

A long silence followed, then Anthrax's "The Devil You
Know" started to play.

I stared into space. What did that mean? Was whoever it
was trying to scare me? I didn't feel particularly scared. It
was all far too weird, first spending several evenings sitting
in silence, breathing into the phone, before finally playing
"The Devil You Know." And there wasn't anything frightening about listening to the disc being taken out and carefully
put back in its case. So it was someone with a CD player.
Who handled their music carefully. It must be a friend, I
thought.

In the end I decided to play "About Today" by the National: "Today, you were so far away," Matt Berninger sang in
his deep, cracked voice.

When I went over to the chocolate bar there was only
one piece left. Where had the rest gone? I looked around as
if expecting to see someone else in the flat.

Just to be sure I went and checked the front door. It was
locked.

"There's someone at the other end," I said to Dansson when I phoned him from work the next morning. "But they don't say anything."

"Are you sure?" he said. "Because sometimes there can be a delay on the line. You know, when you hear your own voice, only much later."

"Hmm," I said. "This isn't like that."

"Maybe it's a sales call," Dansson said.

"It's not a sales call," I said. "It's . . . someone who plays music."

"Music?"

"Yes."

Just before lunchtime I looked up to serve a customer and saw Jallo on the other side of the glass counter. I said hello, but it was impossible to tell if he'd come to see me or just to buy bread. I didn't like him standing so close to the bread with his chapped red fingers, but I had to go to the other end of the counter with another customer to fill a box with vanilla slices, so I didn't say anything. Then, on top of everything else, the customer claimed I'd squashed some icing against the side of the box and demanded that I swap the slice for an undamaged one, so I had to put it back in the display and carefully replace it with another one.

For some reason I happened to look past the customer, and some way off, standing behind a pillar by the tables in the café, I saw a figure in a blue anorak who pulled his head back the moment I looked in that direction.

I could have sworn it was Mr. Magic Bobbi, the magician from the circus.

I looked over to where Jallo had been standing, but could no longer see him. I made an instant decision.

I swung around the end of the counter and set off toward

the pillar. I pushed as fast as I could through the sea of surprised customers clutching their queue tickets as they waited to buy bread.

In a matter of seconds I was at the pillar, flew around it, and collided with a man in late middle age who apologized, even though it was obviously my fault. No Mr. Magic Bobbi.

I mumbled an apology as I looked around. It occurred to me that this was the perfect crowd in which to disappear. A large number of very slow-moving customers wearing a garish array of colors. Like the one good song on a compilation album.

I glimpsed the blue anorak over by the stationery department. The figure's long hair had been tied in a ponytail. I headed toward it, weaving between the café tables. It didn't take long to catch up. I was about to slap my hand on the man's shoulder and ask what the hell he'd done with my friend—I actually had my hand in the air—when I realized that it was clearly someone else. Someone much shorter. Who also happened to be a woman.

I followed her for a short while, and when she stopped at a display of notebooks I pushed past. Mostly because I couldn't just turn round.

I carried on through the doors that led to the underground station, trying to think of a good reason for why I had left work and run off like that. But nothing I came up with sounded even vaguely plausible.

31

"**Do you feel like telling me what happened?**" my boss asked later when we were sitting in his little office to discuss my odd behavior. I thought for a moment and then decided that honesty was probably the best policy after all.

"I thought I saw . . . someone."

He looked at me in surprise.

"What did you say?"

"Someone who . . ."

I hesitated. How was I supposed to explain this in a factual way? I began again, in a slightly more steady voice.

"I thought I saw a magician," I said, nodding slowly as I attempted to adopt a convincing expression. I quickly realized it was hopeless.

Have you ever heard the Bob Dylan song "Hurricane" on the *Desire* album, about the falsely accused boxer? My boss told me off so emphatically that it was all I could think of. I was briefly close to tears. The bow tie was pinching my throat, and I loosened it with a couple of fingers. During the rest of the reprimand I thought about my recurrent dilemma of where to put compilation albums. What do you do with an album featuring two equally big names when it isn't obvious that one of them is making a guest appearance on the other's album? Some are obvious of course: Frank and Nancy Sinatra get filed under Frank. Besides, they're related, which makes the decision even easier. But what about the Traveling Wilburys, for instance? Or *Grimascher och telegram*, which features both Jan Johansson and Cornelis Vreeswijk? Cornelis's name is more prominent on the cover, but it's perfectly obvious that it's a Jan Johansson album.

Jallo was gone by the time I got back to the bakery coun-
ter after my dressing-down. Perhaps he assumed I was going
to be gone for a long time? Perhaps he thought that was how
I usually went for lunch? He doesn't generally have anything against waiting. Either way, he was gone when I got
back. I stood there for a while looking for him before I heard
a familiar remark from the other side of the counter: "Young
man, what do you think you're here for?"

I clicked to bring up another number, then went over to
the woman and took her ticket.

"I'd like to place an order," she said. "And it's rather special, so you'd better fetch a pen and paper."

I fetched the order book from the till.

"I'd like to order a cake. Completely white, like this."

She moved her hands in a circular motion.

"And with a black ribbon around it. And a little peak on
one side. Can you guess what it's supposed to be?"

I shook my head slowly.

According to the roster I finished work at 4 p.m., which meant I could start to get ready at quarter to. If you wiped the counter and did a bit of rearranging toward the end you could manage to spend the last five minutes tucked away in the kitchen. I swept the crumbs and flour from the large marble counter behind the till. Made up some boxes for cakes until I realized I'd done far too many, so I piled the rest up beneath the counter: they could always be used later. Then I rinsed some tongs and tried to avoid serving any more customers for as long as I could by making myself look busy. I checked the time, but it was still only ten to, so I sneaked into the kitchen.

The dishwasher was loaded and running through its cycle. The worktop alongside it was empty. All the cutlery and implements were carefully arranged in the plastic tray next to the sink. I sank onto the little plastic stool by the door. Some of the girls thought the big industrial dishwasher was hard to handle, but I'd learned to use one at the summer camp Jallo and I went to years ago. It was part of the daily routine there for residents to help with the cleaning and washing-up. I used to think it was a pretty easy job even back then.

The last summer at camp Jallo had signed up as one of the leaders.

"Much better," he said. "And you don't have to pay the enrollment fee. Besides, I already know how to do it all. And they say personal experience is a bonus."

Even if he was the same person, it was more like talking to an adult. Suddenly he was taking part in self-awareness sessions and discussing things in a mature way. Asking about my social life, my routines, school, if I still saw Magnus—that sort of thing.

"Isn't there a youth club or something?" he asked.

I shrugged.

"Maybe you could set one up," he said.

I muttered something about that probably being quite hard to do.

"Oh," he said, "you just need to find premises. There must be somewhere that's not being used?"

I shrugged again.

"There must be," he said. "There always is. Look, do you think you could take those headphones off?"

Magnus didn't like Jallo. I don't know why. Maybe he thought he was a slacker. A poseur. Unless he was jealous because we had a different kind of relationship thanks to the summer camp? Maybe he saw him as a potential threat to our friendship. For good reason. Since the business with the Walkman things had settled down a bit. I suppose I'd forgiven him and realized that I was just going to have to accept him for what he was: a coward. But things between us were still frosty. Jallo wasn't particularly pleasant toward Magnus either. One autumn he bumped into us after school.

"Hey, hi there!" he called. "How's it going?"

I had almost reached the post office, where Magnus was waiting, when Jallo ran up to me and pulled my headphones off. I put them back on at once. I could still hear him perfectly well as he walked backward along the pavement ahead of me.

"Do you fancy coming along to a thing with me?" Jallo asked.

"What sort of thing?" I said as we carried on walking awkwardly along.

"Esperanto!" Jallo said breezily. "An Esperanto course!"

"What's that, then?"

I saw Magnus standing in his usual place and slowed down. Jallo continued walking backward ahead of me.

"It's the new global language," Jallo said. "A new language that everyone in the whole world will understand, right? D'you see how cool that would be?! I'm going to do the course. You can come too . . ."

We had reached Magnus now and I nodded briefly in

greeting, but Jallo didn't bother to acknowledge his presence.

"No, I can't," I said. "Magnus and I are—"

"Oh, forget about him," Jallo said wearily. Without so much as looking at him. Without bothering about him at all, in fact.

"Don't you see how brilliant it'll be when the whole world starts talking the same language?" he went on. "You know what this will mean for world peace?"

He leaned closer.

"And you know what an advantage it'll be to know it properly before everyone else?! We'll have one hell of a head start!"

I glanced at Magnus, who was standing right behind Jallo, unassuming as always, unwilling to take up any space.

"Look, Magnus and I are—" I began again.

"Oh! Never mind Magnus!" Jallo groaned.

He took a couple of steps and noticed, entirely without embarrassment, that he was standing right next to Magnus. He looked at me as if he was simply waiting for me to go with him.

"Well?" he said.

Magnus looked down. Waiting for me to made a decision.

"Are you coming or what?" Jallo cried.

I shook my head.

"Fine. Don't, then," Jallo muttered and walked off.

Magnus glared at him as he went. And there we were, together, again.

It annoyed me that Magnus always had to be so defensive. That he always let me make the decisions without contributing anything but a guilty conscience. But he never really wanted much. He never wanted anything new to happen. Everything was supposed to be the way it had always been. As if it was possible to stop time. Which of course it wasn't. In fact he was becoming more and more peculiar. In the end I started to feel uncomfortable in his company.

For him everything was perfectly clear. We were two outsiders who belonged together, and we would always belong with the outcasts and rejects. Naturally I was grateful for his loyalty, but it was starting to feel more and more of a burden.

Perhaps he noticed, because he did try to change as time passed, adopting a rather more provocative tone and suggesting we try more challenging things.

Like the time we walked across the railway bridge. We had been walking all evening without saying much, just wandering about kicking stones. He'd started wearing black clothes and had got hold of that stupid badge, LIVE HARD AND DIE YOUNG. It felt like a hard-rock thing to me. I said as much. Asked if he was planning on becoming a rocker instead. He just grinned and stopped next to the railing.

"Let's climb along the outside," he said.

"What for?"

"Are you too scared?" he said, swinging over the railing.

"Course not," I said.

I climbed over and clung on to the outside of the railing next to him. There was a drop of maybe five or six meters to the railway line. I felt the wind in my hair. In the distance we could hear the train approaching. Magnus looked at me. It was only a game, but I got the feeling that he would have jumped. If I'd asked him to, he would have done it. Without hesitation.

The teachers at Vira Elementary told us to be careful about socializing with kids from other schools. Which basically meant Berg School. Especially if they offered us drugs. Magnus didn't do drugs, but he did develop a sort of unpredictable side to his character. Sometimes I imagined that he came up with things like that to impress me. But in actual fact he just became more and more tragic.

A few weeks later I met Jallo again. By then he'd given up on Esperanto. He said he'd got a part-time job as a buddy at Berg School. Why didn't I visit him there sometime?

I told him that according to Magnus, Berg School was hell on earth, but Jallo said he'd never seen Magnus there.

"Never?" I said.

"Nope," Jallo said.

"Not once?"

He shook his head.

I never broached the subject with Magnus. That was his business. Somehow I had already realized that he didn't spend much time at school. He had a world of his own. He grew less and less engaged in music, and more and more peculiar. He got interested in magic and some homespun version of numerology. He saw a connection between the number of records in a box and good or bad events. He had a weird period when he was interested in magic tricks and magical thinking. He said he was going to become a magician. I tried to explain to him that all magic acts were based on different types of illusion, and that the people who performed them spent hours practicing, but he seemed to think it was more to do with formulas and codes rather than tricking the audience into concentrating on something else. It was like he wasn't at all interested in hearing what I said. Unless he just thought it didn't matter.

He kept coming up with increasingly strange suggestions. Once when we were standing by the marsh he suggested jumping in.

"Let's do it," he urged.

"Are you mad?" I said. "What for?"

"Why not?" he said with a grin.

"Idiot!"

Why not?"

I sighed.

"Because we'd get sucked down and die."

"So?"

I looked at him, but he just glared back with that provocative expression. As if it was all a bit of fun. As if we might as well walk into the marsh and see what happened. No matter what the consequences. As if nothing mattered. As if nothing made any difference.

"You'll have to do it on your own," I said.

"Then you'll be alone."   .

I snorted.

"So? I'd just have to find someone else to hang out with."

"Who?"

I snorted again.

"Anyone," I said.

"You haven't got anyone. Who?"

I shrugged. "Jallo."

"Jallo's an idiot," he said. "He's dangerous. Can't you tell? He doesn't understand anything."

"But you do, I suppose?"

"More than you and him do," he said.

"*He*," I said. "More than you and *he* do."

"Are you the grammar police now, then?" Magnus said.

"No," I said. "That's just the sort of thing you learn if you go to school."

Magnus didn't respond to that.

"Jallo's trying to manipulate you," he said. "Haven't you

noticed? He keeps trying to get you to think you're some-one, you fucking loser."

"Says you, just because you're a loser."

"No more than you and him are."

"You and *he*."

Recently he'd started to adopt a tougher way of talking. It didn't suit him and was just embarrassing. I tried to get him to stop and act normally instead.

Sometimes I wondered if I should tell him what people said about him when he wasn't around. At school. The way they made fun of him. Saying he was crazy and disgusting and an idiot. Not just that, but that he was sick in the head, and that people were scared of him because he'd evidently done all sorts of weird stuff that people loved to talk about.

There were any number of stories about Magnus, each one worse than the last. People were only too happy to gos-sip about him. Not when I was around, obviously. They knew we were friends, so they always stopped the moment I appeared. But I couldn't help hearing anyway—it would have been impossible not to. Magnus was something of a sobering example, a myth. And in a way some of that re-bounded on me. I ended up being automatically associated with him and all the stupid stuff he got up to.

Perhaps I should have said something to Magnus. Tried to make him realize how strange he was getting. Tried to get him to wake up and show him the guy I kept having to protect and look after. But I could never come up with a good enough reason. What good would it do? It would only make him even sadder. Even more alone. Even more weird.

More and more often I found myself wondering what sort of person I would have been if Magnus hadn't existed. Who I might have become if the two of us hadn't hung out together all the time. I could have been someone completely different.

"No, you couldn't," Magnus said. "You are who you are. You can't just become someone else."

"Can't you?" I said. "Surely we choose who we are for ourselves?"

He snorted.

"You're not the type."

"What type?"

"Someone like that . . ."

"I could have been."

"Hardly."

"Just because you get bullied doesn't mean I have to. I could have gone out with Maddy . . ."

"Hardly."

"Why not?"

"Do you know what you are to her?"

He pulled his hand out of his pocket and formed his thumb and forefinger into a zero.

"And how the hell would you know?"

"I just do."

I took a deep breath and leaned my head back against the wall. I looked at the time and realized it was five minutes past four. I pulled the bow tie off and undid my top button. Went off to the changing room, hung up my uniform, and got changed into my own clothes. I put the padlock on my locker, picked up my rucksack, and walked out.

34

Dansson was waiting outside the staff entrance when I came out.

"Do you want to come to Record King?" he said, and I very nearly nodded before I realized that I didn't want to. I was tired of Record King and wanted to try something new. Not that there was anything wrong with Dansson, but hanging out with him every day in the record shop had started to feel like being strapped into the back seat of a car, out of reach of the radio and unable to influence the choice of music.

I wondered if there was any good reason for me not to go. I felt in my pockets and found Jallo's note on the health-food shop receipt.

"I need to find an address," I said and showed him the scrap of paper.

Dansson took it and read.

"Bondegatan 34," he said.

"No," I said. "Bondegatan 3A. That's an A. It's just Jallo's . . ."

I snatched the receipt back.

"Right," Dansson said, sticking his hands in his pockets.

"It's . . . He was in a hurry when he wrote it . . . It's just Jallo's . . ." I said, looking at the writing. "It's supposed to be 3A."

"OK," Dansson said.

I looked at the note again.

"You can see it's supposed to be an A?"

"Sure," Dansson said.

"You can, though, can't you?"

35

Bondegatan 34 was nothing more than a door. In the middle of a wall. No sign. No windows. Just a door, nothing else.

And it was open.

Right inside the door hung a bead curtain, the sort you see in Asian films, usually with a pattern on it. A sunset or a beautiful woman. Walking through it was like walking through water, a slow shower. I let myself be washed by it and emerged on the other side. I found myself standing at one end of a very long corridor with the curtain still swaying behind me.

The walls, ceiling, and floor were covered in dark blue plush. There were small but fairly powerful wall lamps every ten meters or so. I took a couple of steps forward and ran my hand along the soft wall. It felt lovely.

The air smelled of synthetic bananas. Sweets.

I took another couple of steps and realized that walking was surprisingly easy. As if the passageway sloped gently down, extending as far as the eye could see. I walked a bit farther and felt how nice it was to stretch my legs, to let go and stride along.

I carried on down the soft, soundless carpet. The slight slope gave me a bit of extra momentum, and I was swept on by the seemingly endless row of wall lamps. They were relatively bright, but the distance between them was great enough to leave pockets of darkness. You walked out of the light into darkness, then back into light again.

Gravity led me on down the corridor. I just had to keep walking and take long enough strides to stop myself from stumbling.

After a while I started to make out the outline of a door at the other end of the corridor. It looked like an ordinary office door, but as I got closer I saw that it was padded, with round buttons studded across it in a diamond pattern. The handle was wood, perhaps teak. I tried it. The door was locked, but the lock was on my side of the door. I turned the lock and walked into a large dark room with a flickering light in the distance. I could hear soft music. The hall was full of hundreds of people who suddenly burst into synchronized laughter. Blue light enveloped everyone sitting in the auditorium. I turned and reached for the handle to sneak back out again, but the door wouldn't open. The lock was on the other side.

"Don't you see? It's a message?" a voice said in English from the loudspeakers. I decided to walk past all the rows of seats. It got darker again and thunderous music started to play. Before the flight of steps was illuminated by an explosion of light I managed to trip on one of the treads and almost hit my head on the carpet, which smelled of popcorn. I got to my feet, pushed through some swing doors, and emerged into a foyer.

A very short fair-haired man in a red cap nodded to me as he handed a customer their change across the counter. A young man was sitting on a bench beside the popcorn machine, scribbling in one of those free film magazines.

Behind him, a little farther away, stood Dennis.

36

The same broad shoulders and large head. The permed hair was gone, but he still had the same thick, heavy eyebrows. And saggy cheeks. It was definitely Dennis. In one of those cinema uniforms.

I stood by the doors, and the music grew louder again behind me.

The young man on the bench glanced at me idly, toyed with his pen, and appeared so bored by the whole situation that he couldn't help yawning. I noticed that he'd drawn mustaches on Angelina Jolie and Brad Pitt.

The foyer was calm and very quiet. It was warm. The sun was shining through the windows facing the street, dividing the foyer into sunny and shaded areas. The line between them ran across the floor like a boundary. The customer walked off and the very short man went and sat down beside the young man, close enough for me to see that he had gone back to filling in the football pools. I couldn't help noting that he was taking a chance on an away win for Crystal Palace against Arsenal, which seemed pretty risky.

Perhaps he knew something that no one else did? No one was paying much attention to me.

I looked over at Dennis again. It had to be him. It couldn't be anyone else. I closed my eyes for a moment. When I complained to Jallo about all the weird things that only seemed to happen to me, he said that I ought to challenge my own experiences from time to time.

"You can ask the question yourself. Ask yourself: is this really plausible?"

I opened my eyes again. And there he stood. Dennis, the bully who had stolen my Walkman all those years ago. It seemed plausible. In spite of everything. The only particularly odd thing was that someone like Dennis was working in a place like this. A cinema? He ought to be an estate agent or a solicitor, maybe even a doctor by now. I couldn't imagine Dennis's parents congratulating him on getting a job as a cinema usher. But on the other hand, it was a job. An income. Times change. Everything changes. Perhaps something had happened. It often does. He was holding a can of Coca-Cola in one hand, and took a sip as he turned in my direction.

His face froze. He recognized me instantly. We stood there looking at each other, and I realized it was too late to turn away. After a while he raised his head slightly. With the absolute minimum of effort. Barely noticeable and surprisingly calm. He didn't even seem particularly surprised to see me. Almost as if he'd been expecting me to show up. As if he knew I'd be coming. He began to walk toward me. I felt my heart beat faster and had to make a real effort not to run away.

It must have been at least ten, fifteen years since I'd last seen Dennis, at some school thing. Back then I was far too preoccupied with trying to walk straight, not hyperventilate, and show that that sort of reunion wasn't a problem for me. That my time at school hadn't left any scars. I was far too absorbed in my own behavior to notice anyone else. Some of them had their partners with them, I recalled, and I spent an hour or so mingling until I told someone I had to get going. I tried my best to come across as an unbroken individual who had dealt perfectly well with his school days, just in case anyone happened to think otherwise. I walked from group to group with exaggerated calm, raising my plastic glass in toasts and counting the minutes until I could safely escape with a breezy smile glued to my face. I remembered that Dennis had worn an earring. And hadn't his face been a bit fatter even then? Had he looked a bit worn down? I wasn't sure.

Now here he was, standing in front of me holding out his hand. I shook it.

"Hi there!" he said.

I wondered if I had ever held his hand in mine before. It felt soft. Smooth and a bit flabby. Surprisingly limp. There was something subdued and nervous about him. From close up I could see that he had worry lines on his forehead. The last time we met I had been far too self-absorbed to notice him properly, but things were different this time. Did he feel that? Could he tell I was looking at him closely? In a way it was like I was seeing him for the first time. He had a few gray hairs, some crow's feet around his eyes. He had a mole on his forehead that he should probably get checked out. I saw that his shirt collar was a bit too tight around his neck, beneath his bulging double chin. Maybe he was seeing me for the first time too? We stood like that for a while, without saying anything. Those moments were rather strained yet oddly lucid. And possibly more awkward for him.

"Well," he said eventually. "Yeah . . . he said you'd be coming."

"Who did?" I said.

"Jallo."

"You work here?" I asked.

He nodded and took his cap off. Folded and unfolded it a couple of times as if to prove that he had permission to do that. That he didn't have to wear it if he didn't want to.

"Usher," he said. "How about you?"

"Oh," I said, trying to shift my weight nonchalantly to the other leg. "I'm in the bakery business."

He nodded again and took another sip of Coke. It was like we were both trying to normalize the situation and pretend that this wasn't a strangely unreal occurrence at all.

"You got a lot going on now, then?" he said.

I shrugged my shoulders. Didn't know what to say.

"I mean, a lot to do," he went on, stifling a burp.

I didn't know how to respond to this sort of talk. Nothing unusual about that. It occurred to me that I never talked much about work. To be honest, I never noticed much difference in the seasons. You just stood there, pressed the button, and served the customers. I would have liked to have been able to say something funny and smart to prove that I knew a lot about the industry, while simultaneously demonstrating that I wasn't that bothered about it—just that I was aware of it, in spite of the fact that it was him I was talking to.

"Well, of course it's school graduation season," I said eventually. "Lots of cakes . . ."

He nodded knowledgeably, as if he really did know something about it.

"I've got a good idea for a graduation cake," he said.

"Really?" I said.

"Mmm," he said. "Imagine, a white princess cake—"

"Hang on," I said. "Let me guess. With a little black peak—"

"Exactly!" he said, breaking into a grin. "On one side, made of marzipan, so that . . ."

We said it at the same time: ". . . the cake itself looks like a graduation cap!"

He looked delighted.

It could have been far more uncomfortable to find myself eye to eye with Dennis like that. But for some reason it was getting easier and easier with each passing second. I don't know why, but in the end I was almost enjoying standing there. I could have carried on for a good while longer, just looking him in the eye. He looked tired. As if life had treated him roughly. He didn't seem to have anything against standing there like that either. It was clear we weren't going to start socializing. We were never going to be friends. I didn't want that at all. Nor did he, presumably. We weren't going to go out drinking or bowling together. It wasn't the slightest bit dramatic, and the notion that I had once been desperate for his friendship felt very distant indeed. I thought about saying as much to him, but it felt a bit too much. Too big, somehow. And possibly also rather cruel. It was like we'd both woken up from an unpleasant dream and realized that although the waking world may not have been that great, at least it was different from what we thought back then.

He rubbed his hand across his face a few times, screwed his eyes shut, and frowned.

"Look," he said after a while. "I know I'm supposed . . . What's it called? I'm supposed to atone . . ."

"What did you say?" I said.

"Atonement," he said. "What am I trying to say?"

He took a deep breath. Closed his eyes again.

"Look . . . I admit my guilt and would like to apologize for the way we treated you."

He breathed out. Opened his eyes again and looked at me in a way that was both anxious and expectant. I stared at him. Neither of us spoke for what felt like a long time. We stood there in silence. Dennis with his cap in his hand and what he had just said hanging in the air, looking sheepish now, afterward, as if he was expecting some sort of response from me. I almost burst out laughing. What the hell did he mean? Did he really think that we could draw a line under everything, the whole of our teenage lives, and move on? As if it was possible to forgive something like that, to wrap up that whole period, everything that had happened at school, and put it into words. Sort it out, put the pieces back in the right place, and start afresh from the beginning. As if we, if we felt like it, could erase it all and do everything differently.

I just gawked at him. Even so, it was good to hear it, and provided at least some small measure of relief.

After a while of neither of us saying anything he started to glance sideways. As if he was wondering how long this had to go on for and wanted to check the time to see when it could be regarded as done and dusted.

In the end I was the one who broke the silence.

"Can I ask you something?" I said.

He looked at me with those tired eyes as though he had an idea what was coming. As if he had prepared for this. The attack. Revenge. All the difficult questions I was going to ask. He was making a real effort to take responsibility without losing his temper or going to pieces. But I didn't want to ask any of those questions. I wasn't expecting any answers. Not from him. Absolutely not from him. There was only one thing I wanted to know.

"Was it my Walkman?"

Whatever he'd been expecting, this wasn't it. That much was obvious. He looked like he didn't even understand the question.

"What?" he said.

"That's all I want to know," I said. "Was it my Walkman you took?"

"Yes, of course it was," he said. "So, yeah . . ."

I nodded. He nodded back.

"Christ," he went on after a while, giving me a look of pity. "You were so alone. You didn't have anyone."

"Well . . . ," I began to say, "I had . . ."

I suddenly felt that I wanted to get away from there.

"But you were, though," Dennis went on. "You were always utterly alone. It's no fun being on your own. It's fucking horrible. I can see why you wanted your Walkman."

"Oh, it's just . . . I always wondered if it was really mine, or if I was imagining it . . . Jallo suggested that—"

Dennis brightened up.

"Do you go and see Jallo as well?" he said.

I stared at him. Shook my head.

"No . . . He's just a friend of mine."

Dennis looked at me, winked, and nodded. Almost as if we shared a secret. Was he implying something about me and Jallo? If so, what? Maybe he just felt relieved. He certainly looked much less tense now that he'd got the apology out of the way, and it was impossible to tell what he meant by his expression. I felt the urge to get out of there even more strongly now.

"What film are you showing?" I asked.

Dennis glanced toward the cinema.

"Something experimental," he said. "About some friends. Although it's hard to know who the real friend is . . ."

I nodded. I didn't know what to say.

"Is it any good?"

Dennis frowned.

"It's kind of deep," he said with a shrug. "But the music's good. You've always liked music, haven't you?" he said.

He looked happy again, the way you do if you remember something about someone else that makes you look like a more considerate person. Or less arrogant, anyway.

"I listen to quite a lot of stuff myself," he went on when I didn't say anything.

"Oh," I said. "I suppose it's easy these days, with Spotify and SoundCloud and all that."

I glanced at the door. He put his cap back on. It sounded like the end credits were playing inside the cinema.

"Well," he said. "I'd better get back to work, but it would be good to meet up and talk a bit more."

"Hmm," I said. "I'm afraid I don't have a mobile, so—"

"Nor do I," Dennis said. "How about tomorrow? What do you say, dinner at eight?"

37

I left the cinema by the main entrance.

I walked over to the pedestrian crossing on Götgatan and when the light turned green realized that I should actually be going the other way. I turned around and managed to get back to the other side before the lights changed again. I walked until I came to a bus stop, looked up at the sign, and saw that the bus was going my way. So Dennis was seeing Jallo? Why would he be doing that? What did they talk about? Me? Did Dennis have psychological problems? I couldn't help thinking that it was probably his turn to have some now. As if there was some sort of force in the universe that balanced things out. But what had happened in his life to make him think he had to go and see someone like Jallo? And why had he mentioned "Dinner at Eight"?

"You always have to look at new ways of communicating," Jallo once said when we were sitting in his office and he was telling me about some sort of mime course he was thinking of setting up. "Because of course language is mainly just a barrier to understanding." I'd stopped listening to him when he said that sort of stuff a long time ago. I mostly just nodded and agreed with him while I thought about other things.

Eventually the bus showed up, and as soon as I sat down I fell asleep and managed to have one of those dreams that feels like a whole lifetime. Someone was walking behind me and I couldn't see who it was. Just as I was about to turn around I woke up and realized that I'd gone at least three stops too far. I looked out the window and saw that I was right outside the door to Jallo's office. The big illuminated sign was already switched on even though it wasn't quite dark yet. The red and yellow neon letters lit up one after the other, from the bottom, until eventually the man was visible, with the letters forming his hat.

I got off, thinking that I may as well stop in to see Jallo now that I was there. I could take the opportunity to ask him what the hell he was up to.

I went up the narrow stairway with the creaking steps. I kept hold of the handrail because it felt like the wooden steps might give way every time you put your foot down. The receptionist had her face buried in her phone as usual. She didn't bother to pay me any attention, so I didn't say hello to her. I knew my way. I'd been there enough times. I wound my way through the narrow corridors with their bright orange textured wallpaper and the uneven floor that bulged in places and smelled faintly of mold, past the vending machine, following the trail of lights laid out along the edge of the cheap blue carpet. Just before I got to Jallo's office I stumbled over that wretched strip of lights and fell on the floor. I only just put my hands out in time. Jallo looked up from behind the desk in his room.

"Magnus?" he said with a look of surprise.

He came out and helped me to my feet. He brushed me down and carried my rucksack into the room. He turned his arm to look at his watch.

"I'm seeing a client in twenty minutes, but grab a seat and we can have a quick chat."

I followed him into the small, windowless office, tucked between the toilets and the recycling bins.

38

He folded a newspaper that was lying open on the desk. Waved it in the air.

"Interesting article here," he said. "They've come up with a new way to measure happiness. They're going to debate it at the United Nations. *Happiness.* Can you imagine? Ridiculous."

He laughed and shook his head. I sat down on the chair on the other side of the desk.

"All nonsense, obviously, if you read between the lines. But you have to admire their nerve. Pushing it as far as that, I mean. Like they say, 'The bigger the lie . . .'"

He tossed the newspaper on the floor, picked up a pen, and put the top back on. He leaned back.

"So, my friend," he said.

I ran my hands along the armrests.

"What's all this business with Dennis?" I said.

He put the pen to his lips and tapped it a few times without replying.

"Why did you send me to see him?"

He still didn't say anything. Just looked at me with that lazy, inscrutable gaze.

"You knew he'd be there, didn't you? At Bondegatan 34?"

He threw his arms out.

"I thought it would be good for you to meet," he said at last. "Good for both of you."

I leaned back and heard music playing very faintly from the computer in the middle of the desk. The same old Sinatra playlist that Jallo always played. The very worst way to listen to music: a barely audible carpet of background noise that you really had to concentrate on if you wanted to make out any of the details. How could he bear it? He must have it on the lowest possible setting. I stopped mid-movement and tried to sit as silently as I could.

I was well aware that some music has the ability to put me into a trance-like state. I did things without thinking about it. Or imagined that I was doing things that never actually happened. Jallo had once pointed that out to me, and had suggested that I try applying that plausibility test of his. So this sort of music that you could hardly hear always felt a bit sneaky. I wanted to know what sort of music was being played so I could figure out how it affected me.

"I gave him your number a while back," Jallo said. "But I don't suppose he could bring himself to call you. I've asked him several times, but he keeps saying he hasn't got around to it. Then he said that he had called, but hadn't dared say anything. He said he'd call the following week, but a week later he said the same thing. So I thought it would be just as well to send you to see him. Did it go OK, then?"

"What?" I said, suddenly thinking that perhaps I ought to have been listening to him and not the music. So I tried to remember what he'd said and listen. Sometimes you can hear what someone has already said: as if the words still hang in the air for a while, and you can pick them up after they've been spoken.

"Seeing him again?" he asked.

I raised my head and stared at his sly-looking face. That little smile that kept playing at the corners of his mouth.

"I suppose so," I said.

He nodded thoughtfully. Looked at me intently, as if he was waiting for me to say something else. Perhaps I ought to. After all, I was the one who'd raised the subject. I didn't know why though, now. I looked around the room.

"He's scared," I said.

"What of?" Jallo said.

"Of me."

"Why is he scared of you?"

"I don't know. There's just something about me."

"What?"

I shook my head.

"I don't know. Something. What about you?"

"Me?" Jallo said.

"Yes."

"Oh, there's nothing about me."

"Why would you and him be seeing each other, then?"

"*He*," Jallo said.

"What?"

"You mean, you and *he*."

We looked at each other for a few moments. Jallo sat there quietly, smiling, as if he was waiting for me or had taken a vow of silence or something. It felt like it was my turn to talk.

"He said it was my Walkman," I eventually said.

"Your what?" Jallo said.

"Don't worry; it doesn't matter," I said.

Sinatra was singing "In the Wee Small Hours of the Morning," and I could just make out the lyric about a lonely heart learning the lesson.

I took a deep breath and tried to get back to the conversation.

"Why did you tell me where to find Dennis when you knew I was looking for Magnus?" I said.

Jallo tapped his pen against his lips. Then he put it down on the desk and rubbed his face with both palms.

"I gave you an address I thought you needed," he said.

"What does that have to do with Magnus?"

He leaned back in his chair. Blew out his cheeks and let the air slowly escape from his mouth.

"Well," he said. "Nothing."

"Nothing?"

He shook his head.

"OK, then," I said. "Look, this business with Magnus is driving me mad. I can't figure out where he's gone."

Jallo nodded. The song came to an end, and "Learnin' the Blues" started to play instead.

"I can't help worrying," I went on, shifting in the chair. I leaned over one armrest, but that wasn't at all comfortable, so I sat back the way I'd been sitting before.

"And then there's the thing with the phone," I said. "Someone keeps calling me."

"Oh?"

Jallo raised his eyebrows in that nonchalant way, as if he wasn't the least bit taken aback but still wanted to look surprised.

"Yes," I said. "Which is kind of OK, I guess . . . We play each other records."

"You play *records*?"

"Yes! But I don't think it's Magnus."

"Why not?" he said.

"It doesn't feel like him."

"No?" Jallo said, nodding thoughtfully.

He leaned his head back and looked up at the ceiling. He tapped his pen against the desk in time to Sinatra.

"Look, to be honest I don't know that much about Magnus," Jallo went on.

"Oh?"

"Seeing as I've never met him."

He stopped tapping the pen and made a vague gesture with the other hand. I watched him. Tried to work out what he meant.

"Yes, you have," I said.

He looked me in the eye and shook his head.

"Of course you have," I said. "You always say—"

"I know what I always say," he interrupted. "I can't help having an opinion about him, based on what you've told me. But I've never actually met him."

"Yes, you have . . . The two of you—"

"When?" he interrupted again. "Give me one occasion when I met him."

I had to laugh. I opened my mouth to speak but couldn't think of what to say. My laugh sounded nervous. I could hear that for myself.

"Well, the other day," I said eventually.

"No," he said, shaking his head. "You were standing in your doorway, and you said you'd seen him. I never saw him."

"OK, a long time ago, then. Back at school."

He shook his head again.

"You went to the same school as him," I said.

"So you keep saying. But he was never there."

We were both sitting upright now. Our eyes locked together.

"He was," I said.

"Not as far as I'm aware," he replied.

"OK, maybe not in class, but afterward . . ."

Jallo was still shaking his head.

"I've never met him," he said.

"Well," I said. "He's not exactly the sociable type."

Jallo picked up his pen again and tapped it against his

lips. I took a deep breath. Leaned back as relaxed as I could and tried to breathe normally. I felt like I needed to hold on to something. Jallo waved the pen in the air as if he was wafting a strand of hair or mote of dust away.

"You know what I think?" he said, and the pen stopped moving. "I think you should stop worrying about him."

There are some things you just know. If anyone were to ask "How do you know that?" you'd reply "I just do." It's as obvious as the sky being gray and the grass brown. If the weather's been bad and the summer dry. The question itself seems almost provocative. Something similar happened when Jallo leaned back in his fancy office chair, the one he loved to rock backward and forward in, with his elbows on the armrests and his fingertips touching under his chin. There was something ridiculous about the whole situation. Even so, somehow he had managed to get to me, and I was breathing fast.

"What are you trying to say?" I said.

"I'm just saying what I see," Jallo said.

"This is absurd," I said. "Magnus . . . Magnus is just Magnus."

He held the palms of his hands up, and moved them up and down as if he were weighing something in them.

"So tell me," he said, swiveling in his chair again. "Does it seem plausible?"

I snorted. I tried desperately to think of something smart to say to put a stop to this ridiculous situation.

"If you stop and think about it . . . ," Jallo went on, "doesn't it seem a bit strange that you've both got the same name?"

"What's strange about that?" I said.

"It's a remarkable coincidence, though, isn't it?"

"I'm called Magnus, and so are lots of other people. Plenty of people have the same name."

He nodded.

"But . . . don't you think it was very convenient that he first showed up all those years ago just when you needed him most?"

I shrugged.

"That was a good thing, wasn't it?" I said.

"And then he vanished when you put him to the test."

"OK," I said. "That wasn't quite so good."

"Why didn't he stand up for you then, that time with Dennis, when you really needed him?"

I felt myself getting angry. What did he know about Magnus? What did he know about what he was like?

"He couldn't," I said. "OK? He just couldn't!"

"Fine," Jallo said, holding his hands up as if in surrender. "I'm not trying to force you to see things a particular way. But perhaps you could try thinking about it."

I got to my feet. Anger had freed something inside me. It felt almost refreshing. I glared at Jallo and tried to maintain the accusatory tone in my voice.

"That he doesn't exist, you mean?" I said.

Jallo didn't answer. He didn't nod. He didn't move at all. He just sat there looking at me calmly as I stood there breathing hard.

"That he's *never* existed?" I went on.

He shrugged as if we were talking about something random, like a PIN number or a postcode.

"You could try it out as an idea," he said, then reached back so that his elbow touched the red velvet curtain behind him. It was sloping. The whole room was sloping.

"Are you saying that the circus never existed either, then?" I said after a pause.

Jallo peered at the window.

"I don't know. I'm sure you know better than anyone."

Jallo raised one of his fingers to his mouth and bit the nail. He pulled a face and stopped. He opened the top drawer of his desk and very carefully pulled on a pair of bright white cotton gloves.

"Maybe try looking at it like this," he said after a while. "We become new people all the time."

"What do you mean by that?"

"We change. There's nothing odd about that."

I found myself looking at the dresser and standard lamp in the corner, on top of the handwoven rug. The extension cord was curled up beside them.

"We try to create order," Jallo eventually said. "But the natural state is chaos. You know what Shakespeare said?"

"No. What did he say?"

" 'All the world's a circus'!"

" 'A stage,' surely?" I said.

Jallo waved one white-gloved hand in the air impatiently.

"Doesn't matter," he said. "That's what he meant, anyway . . ."

He looked tired, as if he was trying to bring the discussion to an end, but suddenly he raised his eyebrows and held one gloved finger up in the air as if he'd just thought of something funny. He turned and hunted through his drawers. He pulled out a cable, then a red microphone, and held it up in front of me.

"Karaoke?"

40

After a while I began to hear the sound of voices out in the waiting room. Jallo cleared his throat. He put the microphone away and glanced at the door, stood up, walked over, and closed it. As he did, I noticed the full-length mirror on the back of the door. When he started to close the door, only the table, part of the floor, and the bookcase at the other end of the room were visible in it. But as the door closed, first my clothes then more and more of me came into view in the mirror. Once it was shut I was standing there.

Jallo went back to his chair. He closed the drawer containing the karaoke equipment, sat back down and reached over the desk, and dropped his pen into the desk tidy.

"So what happened at work?" he said.

"What?" I said, looking at myself in the mirror.

"The other day. You ran off."

I nodded.

"It was Mr. Magic Bobbi," I said, still staring at my own reflection in the door.

Jallo frowned.

"Who's Mr. Magic Bobbi?" he asked.

"And you were there," I said.

"Yes," Jallo said.

I could sense him leaning toward me even though I couldn't see him.

"Magnus, your imagination is a great asset," he said. "It's a gift. You just need to learn how to manage it. Do you understand? You need to learn how to use it properly. Think of it like this—you're like a superhero who just needs to learn to control his superpowers."

I looked at myself in the mirror. Raised one arm slightly, as if to make sure that the arm in the mirror moved at the same time. It did. It waved. That was plausible. It was all plausible. Even so, it still felt like I'd walked into a dream world. Where everything worked differently. It was as if words meant different things now. Unless they meant the same as before but in a different way. Unless they meant exactly the same things they had always meant, but that I had always thought they meant something else. I felt I ought to say something in order to stop myself from going completely mad.

"But . . . ," I began. "What about the person who keeps phoning me? Do you think that really happened?"

Jallo shrugged his shoulders.

"Once again," he said, "does it seem plausible?"

I didn't say anything for a while.

"Someone's definitely playing stuff," I said.

"Playing?" Jallo said.

"Music. There's someone at the other end playing music."

Jallo frowned.

"Mmh . . . no," he said, shaking his head. "That sounds odd."

"But I can hear it," I said.

Jallo nodded slowly.

"Yes," he said. "But who the hell would be playing music for you?"

41

The phone rang again not long after I got home. I let it ring a few times, properly listening to the sound. I heard it echo in the room, so I was sure it was real. When I pressed the green button to take the call, neither of us said anything at first. Almost like a greeting. As if we both wanted to assure ourselves that the same rules—no words, just music— still applied. I clutched the receiver extra hard. Tapped it gently with my fingertips to make absolutely sure this was really happening. I decided to wait this time. Let him start. If nothing happened, then so be it. But I didn't have to wait long before I heard a click of a disc being inserted.

"Here I Go Again" by Whitesnake.

When it was finished I held the receiver up to the speaker and played the short instrumental piece "I Know You" by Dislocated Timeline, from *Memories from Tuesday*. (He could always google it if he didn't know it. Or use one of those music apps that tell you the artist and title with a minimum of effort. If they actually covered a track like that. I wasn't going to make things easy for him.)

After it finished there was a bit of crackling on the line,

then he played "How Do You Feel" by Jefferson Airplane. I thought that was a bit unimaginative. I let out a deep and very audible sigh. So that the person at the other end would realize that I thought he needed a bit more instruction.

I responded with "This Is Hardcore" by Pulp.

He played Metallica's "Sad But True," which I reluctantly had to admit had a good, heavy intro and stirring verses. The bridge was OK as well, but the chorus wasn't up to much. I replied with "U Think U Know, But U Have No Idea" by Eps. In response I got "All That I Have Done Wrong" by P-Dust, which—as far as I was aware—only existed on SoundCloud and possibly some obscure website. That made me think. There weren't many people who knew about P-Dust. And it was almost as far from hard rock as you could get. Impressive. A bold move. Unconventional. But the more I thought about it, the more I realized that the combination wasn't all that unthinkable. In a way it was perfect, because it was as elegant as it was unexpected. On my shelf P-Dust would have stood a long way from both Eps and Pulp, but now that I had heard it with my own ears, I saw the connection. It struck me that the choice between A and B could just as well be C.

I played Ben Wilson's "What Will Happen Next."

He played Robert Palmer's "Can We Still Be Friends?"

Tasteless. But still. Something had happened.

I responded with Andrew Bayer's instrumental "All This Will Happen Again." Daring, I know, but sometimes you have to take a risk. I was feeling courageous.

He replied with "It's Going to Be Fine" from the same album. I sat there listening to the calm, repetitive piano music and synthesized voices. Looked out through the window. It was raining outside. Once again I found myself looking at the advertisement showing the guy in his underwear. The tear was even bigger now. Like a big, heart-shaped hole.

"It's Going to Be Fine" had finished a while back, and I quickly dug out Erik Ruud's "How Can You Be So Sure?" and played it.

There was a long silence at the other end, then some rustling and clicking sounds. And then: "Fix You" by Coldplay.

42

The next day there was a letter lying on the doormat. I knew at once what it was. I took it to the kitchen table. Got myself a bowl of cereal. Opened the envelope and read the letter, written in that familiar handwriting.

Dear Magnus!

Probably easiest to reach you with a letter.
I just wanted to say—thanks for everything.

> *Best wishes,*
> *Magnus*

I turned the sheet of paper over and scrutinized it. That was all there was. I read the strange note three times. Sat for a while looking out the window, then read it a fourth time. In the end I put it on the pile of mail next to the fridge. I didn't have time for that sort of thing just then. I had to plan my selection of music for that evening's phone call.

About the Author

JONAS KARLSSON (b. 1971) writes plays and short fiction. One of Sweden's most prominent actors, Karlsson has performed on Sweden's premier stage and in several acclaimed feature films and television series. In 2005, Karlsson made his debut as a playwright, earning rave reviews from audiences and critics alike. Spurred by the joy of writing for the stage, Karlsson began writing fiction. With an actor's ear for the silences that endow dialogue with meaning and a singular ability to register moods and emotions, Jonas Karlsson has blossomed into one of Scandinavia's finest literary authors, with two novels and three short story collections published to date. He has been awarded with the Ludvig Nordström Award 2018 for his short story collections *The Second Goal, The Perfect Friend,* and *The Rules of the Game.*

About the Type

This book was set in Berkeley, a typeface designed by Tony Stan (1917–88) in the early 1980s. It was inspired by, and is a variation on, University of California Old Style, created in the late 1930s by Frederic William Goudy (1865–1947) for the exclusive use of the University of California at Berkeley. The present face, in fact, bears influences of a number of Goudy's fonts, including Kennerley, Goudy Old Style, and Deepdene. Berkeley is notable for both its legibility and its lightness.